A King Production presents…

Lovin' Thy Enemy

A Novel

Joy Deja King
FAITH WEATHERS

Cover concept by Joy Deja King
Cover model: Joy Deja King

Library of Congress Cataloging-in-Publication Data;
A King Production

Lovin' Thy Enemy/by Joy Deja King and Faith

For complete Library of Congress Copyright info visit;
www.joydejaking.com
Twitter @joydejaking

A King Production
P.O. Box 912, Collierville, TN 38027

A King Production and the above portrayal log are trademarks
of A King Production LLC

This Book is Dedicated To My:

Family, Readers, and Supporters.
I LOVE you guys so much. Please believe that!!

—Joy Deja King

Dedication:

I want to thank God for blessing my imagination and loving me through the process. Every word I write is dedicated to My Father Rev. Earl R. Cheek, my sister Tanya Cheek, Lil Faith, my first-born Sean Cheek and my beloved mother Cindory Cheek. RIP and keep an eye on your girl.

I must acknowledge my children Courtney, Jada, Anaia, and Avery. We have all made sacrifices for me to live my dream. I love you! My mentor Eros aka David Bradshaw, Thank you for your friendship and guidance, Love ya! To Linda Williams (the voice in my head) Lol! Love you! And most definitely Joy Deja King for giving me this opportunity to rock it out with you. Much appreciation!

To my readers thank you for riding with me through each book and every crazy character. Much Love!

--*Faith*

"I'm The Only Lady Here, Still The Realest Nigga
In The Room."

~*Beyonce*~

A KING PRODUCTION
Lovin' Thy
Enemy
A NOVEL
JOY DEJA KING
FAITH WEATHERS

Chapter 1

Charly

I love hard and there's not a damn thing wrong with it. I am who I am and nothing or nobody is going to change that. When you grow up as the only child of an original gangster like Charlie Brinx, you learn to go hard or take yo' punk ass home.

My daddy owned the streets for over three decades. Even when he did Fed time, his name alone made niggas piss in their pants. And when he came out, he took over the streets again. You name it, my daddy did it and nobody did it better than Charlie Brinx.

So, hell yeah I'm hard. These niggas don't respect a weak ass bitch. Not in this game anyway, and not in life period. Daddy taught me everything he knew and being his only child, all power fell into my lap because I'm the only one he trusts.

I carry a weight on my shoulders most men couldn't handle. Daddy wanted a boy to carry on his legacy but he got me instead. Hence the name Charly, named after the OG himself. He probably wanted to have more children but soon after my birth, my mother was diagnosed with cancer. She tried her best but succumbed to the deadly disease by the time I was three. So yeah, I'm a daddy's girl. It wasn't all sunshine and roses either. Daddy pushed me to be better, smarter, quicker and more driven then the rest. Although I became a teenage mother, I didn't let that stop me. I stayed on my grind and gained my father's respect.

Cancer took my mother, now that fucker has come again to claim my daddy but he's fighting it. It's a secret that no one in the organization knows anything about. His enemies would pounce on his territory if they knew. Hell, his friends would too but not on my watch.

I sipped my Butterscotch Frappuccino inside Starbucks going over the books on my laptop when I saw him. He walked in and flashed a smile at me but I dropped my head pretending not to notice. I picked up my phone and opened the camera to scrutinize my appearance. My long hair was draped over my left shoulder. Lips were poppin', thanks to the high-shine gloss. The extra-large diamond hoop earrings brought just enough bling and my matte gold and black sunglasses set my look off. Feeling confident from the neck up, I placed my phone down and glanced over my attire. I was dressed in my signature all black everything, black blouse, black jeans and knee high black boots. My girls were sitting pretty making my cleavage play peek- a- boo. My golden complexion set off the black ensemble like a piece of new, fresh out the box jewelry. Yeah, I was beautiful and that's not being conceited, it's just something my daddy drilled in my head from the time I was little. He told me I was a beauty, so I believed him. Why wouldn't I since he married my mother. My dad always kept pictures of her around and I thought she was the epitome of perfection, even after she loss all of her hair due to her illness. After briefly reminiscing about my mother, my attention went back to the man who made my heart skip a beat for a second.

I heard he was back but this was my first time laying eyes on him since I was sixteen years old. I wondered if he even recognized me after all this time. I went back to work as if he wasn't standing a few feet away.

The barista called his name to pick up his coffee. Damn he was still fine. He was one of the few people I knew who had jet black eyes, except my daughter Cadence that is. Cross was mixed with black and Italian. His complexion looked as if he'd been eternally kissed by the sun. His eyes had this way of putting you in a trance. Time had been good to him. Standing 6'2, solid build about 220 lbs, his hair was cut short in the front and tapered in the back. His neatly trimmed facial hair made his lips appear even more succulent. *Damn his lips looking all soft and shit. Focus Girl!* I screamed to myself while staring at my laptop trying to concentrate, when I heard my name.

"Charly?"

I looked up and there he was standing in front of me looking like an Adonis.

"I thought that was you. You haven't changed a bit."

The smile on his face was making my kitty throb. *Stop that shit!* I wanted to pat her to make her behave. Instead I gave my infamous resting bitch face expression.

"It's me, Cross." He slightly raised his eyebrow, like he was offended I didn't recognize him.

"Oh, Cross long time no see." I didn't crack a smile. The hoe in me, that rarely if ever came out, was dying to make an appearance. *Please go away before I crawl across this table and straddle your fine ass. The self-control I thought I had mastered was testing my soul.*

"You're still mean as hell." Cross chuckled.

"I guess....." I shrugged my shoulders, giving the best, your thoughts are irrelevant to me aura.

"Well I see you're busy. I just wanted to say hi. It's good seeing you."

"Yeah you too." And with that I watched him walk out of my life again.

Cross Payne and I grew up like family. His

father Curtis and my daddy were best friends since childhood. They got in the game together. They were partners, both were ruthless and no one dared to fuck with the C&C Crew. But just like a tragic hood movie, money, power and friendship don't mix. And to hear my daddy tell it, Curtis set him up so he could take complete control over the C&C Crew. Then the street wars began. Their soldiers had to choose sides. The blood shed was ridiculous. So much heat was brought down, that Francesco, the Italian head of the entire organization called a meeting demanding a truce between the two. They obliged but the once best friends never spoke again.

It wasn't until my senior year, when at a classmate's summer kick back, that Cross and I would see each other again. It was awkward at first and we tried our best to make nice. By the end of the night, we were both lit and talked for hours before ending up in my classmate's parent's bed. I was a virgin and very protective over who would pop my cherry but lust and being tipsy got the best of me. Cross made unadulterated, passionate love to me for hours. Shit was so good I cried. We didn't think about the consequences it was just us, and it was amazing. Until the next day, when I found out Cross had gone back to Arizona to begin his sophomore year of college. No goodbye or nothing. I felt dumb and depressed because I had broken some of my daddy's most important rules. Never let your guard down and stay away from the Payne's. If you see them walking down the street, cross that damn street because they cannot be trusted. And the biggest one, don't give up the goodies.

Needless to say, my dad was ready to kill me when he found out I was pregnant and I wouldn't tell him who the father was. He didn't utter more than three words to me for most of my pregnancy. If it wasn't for my grandmother, Big Mama and my best friend Tia, I don't know what I would've done. But the day I gave birth to Cadence, everything changed. My dad fell in love with her and he became her world.

I slammed my laptop close. Reliving that time of my life made me pissed the fuck off all over again, as if the foul shit just happened yesterday. I had to go see Tia, to fill her in. I keep my circle small and I really keep my circle of trust even smaller, but Tia is my day one.

Tia was helping a customer when I came in, so I browsed the store to see what new arrivals she had got in.

She was in her element when it came to all things fashion and style. Tia's short cut perfectly framed her heart shaped face. Her copper complexion glowed as usual. She was a tiny thing standing 5'6 120lbs. My girl was the personification of sexy. The men loved her and women hated her until they got to know her. Then they were just jealous or adored her like I did. She could have any man she wanted but she was a free spirit. Tia was also a girlie girl. She loved makeup, clothes and shoes...in that order. She parlayed her passion for shoes into a booming business. She opened Tia's Shoe Heaven five years ago after getting a master's in business and finance. My bestie was smart and beautiful.

"Thank you and come again." Tia waved bye to the customer. She walked over to me grinning. "Hey girl, what brings you here, shouldn't you be at work making men shake in their boots?" she teased.

"I should be but girl I'm the one shaking in my boots."

"Ah hell! I need to hear this." Tia dragged me over to the fuchsia sofa she had by the window. "Now what happened?"

"You know I go to Starbucks every morning. Well guess who walks in while I'm in there, grinning from ear to ear and shit?"

Tia's eyes widened, "Girl who?"

"Cross Payne!"

"Shut up! Are you serious? I told you I had heard he was back but I thought it was just a street rumor."

"Well it's true." I rolled my eyes.

"So, what happened? Did he see you? How did he look? What did you say? Girl, what you gonna do?" Tia rambled off question after question.

"Damn bitch slow down!" I laughed at my crazy friend. "Yes, he saw me, he walked over to me and spoke. I played it off though. You know I had my can't be bothered frown plastered across my face but girl he looked so damn fine. I was tempted to go make another baby wit' that nigga...I'm playin'. But seriously, years have passed and he still gets to me."

Tia shook her head. "Honey, if it was me, that's exactly what we would be doing. Making up for lost time by having the best sex of our lives."

I hit her arm. "Oh shut up! But anyway, we exchanged pleasantries and he left."

Tia made a face. "That's it? You didn't get his number?"

"Nope!" I rolled my eyes at Tia.

"Charly, you know I love you right? But you fuckin' up. This is not the time to be hardcore. He's your first love and you could get a second chance with him."

I turned my lips up at Tia. "Take ya love story ass on somewhere. Did you forget he left and never looked back? Nah you didn't forget because it was you who held my hand during my pregnancy not him."

"A pregnancy he didn't know anything about either, Charly. You can›t blame him for that."

I sucked my teeth and turned my head and stared out the window. Tia did have a point. "Yeah I know but it's kinda hard to tell a guy who's living his life in college. Who may even have a girlfriend, your one night of passion led to a baby on the way."

"So now what?"

I turned back to face Tia. "Nothing, life goes on," I shrugged. "Nothing has changed. No one can ever know that he's Cadence's father. It would kill daddy but not before he killed Cross."

Tia tell let out a long sigh. "I think you need to tell him about Cadence. He will love her and Candy has a right to know her daddy. Plus, it's bound to come out especially if they run into each other. There's no denying, she has her daddy's eyes. It's a damn shame a father and daughter are being kept apart because of a vendetta that has been going on for too long."

"It is what it is." I stood up. "A'ight chicky, I gotta get to work."

"Charly, why don't you get out the game while you still can? I know you've stacked plenty of bread. With as many businesses your family has, it should be easy to go legit."

I remained silent for a second taking in what Tia said. "I get your point but the old man still has a say."

"What about Cadence? She'll be 18 in two years. Do you really want her joining you in the organization?" Tia pointed her finger at me, being so damn dramatic with her hand gestures.

"You think I haven't thought about that?" I snapped.

Tia threw her hands up. "A'ight, I'm just trying to help. I know you love this lifestyle, it's all you know but I worry about you. That's what friends do."

"I know. I apologize for snapping at you," I said giving Tia a hug.

"You know I love you, girl." Tia always told me she loved me whenever we parted ways, or before getting off the phone.

"Back atcha!" That was my typical response to Tia expressing her love. She was the complete opposite of me. She was the calm to my crazy. "Talk to you later." I called out as I left the store.

Chapter 2

Cross

After all this time, I finally saw Charly again. Thinking about her put a smile on my face. But instead of me taking advantage of us running into each other and asking for her number, so we can stay in touch, I walked away. Kinda how I did all those years ago. Back then I was a youngin', now I'm a grown ass man, so what's my excuse. I need to see her again. This time I won't make the same mistake.

The car behind me kept honking his horn, interrupting my thoughts. "A'ight! A'ight!" I threw my hand out the window and pulled up to the drive thru. "Pick up for Lita Payne."

I picked up my mom's prescriptions and headed to the house. I hated seeing her so frail. Early Alzheimer's was setting in and she needed around the clock care. Which my father proudly did. He catered to my mother's every need.

The twenty-minute drive to my father's estate gave me time to think. My mind went from Charly, to my mother and now I was thinking about how much I missed my kids. I couldn't wait for the summer so they could come stay with me. Then I remembered I needed to call the realtor. I love my pops and all but I needed my own space.

When I pulled onto the grounds the extra security made my antennas go up. "Yo, what's the problem?" I asked the guard Melvin, slowing down.

"Salvador was gunned down in broad daylight," he informed me.

"Not Sal! Dammit!" I pounded my fist down hitting the wheel so hard, I thought I felt something pop.

"I know. We're all taking it hard. Everybody has to lay low until the family meeting."

"Oh, fuck!" My frustration grew by the moment.

"Orders came down from Francesco himself. Sorry." Melvin shrugged his shoulders.

I drove on in and parked. I noticed both of my brother's SUV's in front. Now we were all stuck on the estate for I don't know how long. My irritation was at an all-time high. I caught myself taking it out on my car door as I slammed it shut.

I could smell my Pop's cigar as soon as I entered the foyer. The smell was coming from his office. "Pop!" I banged on the door before opening it.

Pop was leaning against his desk. I saw my brothers Santi and Curtis Jr. sitting there.

Curtis Jr. was covered in so many tattoos that you would think he was a completely different complexion than he was. His skin color was barely visible underneath all the body art. In my opinion, it was over the top but that was my brother for you, over the top. Now, Curtis Jr. was the spitting image of Pops. They were the same height 6'1. Where Pops age had turned some of his muscle into fat, Curtis Jr. was a solid 225lbs. His arms were straight guns.

Santiago on the other hand favored my mother more, kind of like me. We had the jet black curly hair. I kept mine cut short but Santi's hair was long. He reminded me of a lion when it was all out. Santi was more of a lover not a fighter. But he had no need to fight because Curtis Jr. was crazy enough for all of us. Santi was more reserved, always wanting to impress Pops. He could've gone far on the basketball court standing 6'3 but he never focused on much of anything too long other than women that is. Which is why he had five kids by four different women. The ladies loved Santi and he loved them too.

"We on lockdown for real, Pops?" I took a seat in the oversized leather chair.

"You know the routine. We can't put all the other families at risk." Pop got up and walked around to his chair and sat down.

"Sal was a good dude too," Santi said, shaking his head.

"Francesco is not going to rest until whoever is behind this is dealt with." Pop relit his cigar.

"I don't blame him, I'm ready!" Curtis Jr.

barked, getting riled up like he always did. "If we need to go to war, then so be it."

"I'ma go check on Ma." I did want to go see my mother but I also wanted an excuse to make an exit. I couldn't take being in the room any longer. Curtis Jr. was a hothead with a big mouth. Personally, I didn't have a clue how he was still breathing because he was always into some bullshit.

I left out hoping to spend some time alone with my mother but she was sleeping. She looked so peaceful. Not wanting to wake her, I stood for a few minutes and watched her resting before I went to my room and got online to look for a new place to live.

"Cross!"

"Yeah Pop, come in."

"The meeting is tonight at eight. I want you to go with me. It's time I let them know, you'll be stepping up to take over running things."

"Pop, you know Curtis Jr. is gonna lose it."

"He'll deal with it. His temper is the reason I can't have him controlling the organization. You're a thinker and your brother just reacts. He needs to focus on his pending court case anyway. How can I choose him when he's about to do time? I didn't get this far making stupid deci-sions."

"I hear you. We'll soon see how this plays out. Oh, I got Ma's medicine." I got up and handed Pop the bag. "She was sleeping and I didn't wanna wake her."

"Today was rough for her. I had to make her eat." My father sighed.

"I love my mother more than anything but no one will blame you, if you decide she'll get better care in a home."

"This is her home! She needs to be here, with her family, surrounded by her own things. This is not up for discussion, so don't bring it up again," Pop warned, storming out the room.

I didn't want to argue with my father. I knew he loved our mother but he was in denial about how bad her condition was. Just yester-day she thought I was my brother Andrew who died when he was 9 years old. When it came to my mother, Pop let his heart rule his decisions. I get it but damn, he's going to run himself ragged taking care of her. I guess that's what love does to a man.

My parents had been to hell and back just to be together. Francesco hired Pops back in the day to protect his favorite niece, my mother Lita but what he didn't do, was expect them to fall in love. Francesco had my father beat to an inch of his life but when my Pops kept getting back up, Francesco respected that, so he didn't kill him. But when he found out my mother was pregnant, he wanted them both dead. Instead, Francesco hid my mother away at a catholic home for unwed mothers. My dad wouldn't give up though. He and his best friend at the time Charlie, tracked my mother down and got her out of there. That also impressed Francesco. He felt my Pops had heart, so he not only put him to work but also gave them his blessing to get married.

"Oh, shit! I think I found my new home!" I shouted. Ready to put thinking about my parent's forbidden love story in the back of my mind for a minute. "This penthouse on Walton Street is what I been looking for!" I said out loud, excited that I found the perfect spot, so I could escape the confines of this house.

Chapter 3

Charly

The news of Sal getting murdered made its rounds on the streets. I was sitting at my desk when Francesco's other son Luca called. My heart went out to him and his family. Sal was a good dude and he didn't deserve to die like that. Luca and I talked for a while. We had that kind of relationship. For years on and off he and I spent a lot of heated nights together. Tia always thought we would end up together but I knew different. There was no way his father would condone him being in a relationship with a black woman. Although Francesco treated us like family we knew what time it was. So, we settled on being secret lovers and it was cool with me. I wasn't looking to settle down anyway.

I pulled up to my father's house to make sure he was straight. This lock down was going to drive me crazy so I asked Tia to pick up Cadence and let her spend the night with her. I had to listen to her go on and on about this being a sign I needed to get out of the game. Blah, blah, blah, I didn't feel like hearing that shit so I told her I had to go. I ran to the store real quick to pick up some groceries. The last lockdown lasted three days.

"Hey, Daddy!" I kissed him on the cheek when I entered the living room.

"Hey, baby girl. I was just about to call you. I was getting worried with the lockdown going on."

"I stopped at the store to get us something to eat. Remember what happened last time."

"Well, if you had called your old man, you would've known there's a meeting tonight with the families at 8."

"Sorry, Daddy but at least you got food," I said, going into the kitchen to put the groceries away.

"Charly, I would've done that for you. I was getting the rooms ready for you and Cadence." Miss Erma looked around. "Where is my pretty girl anyway?"

"She's spending the night with Tia. I thought it was best considering."

"I was hoping to see her. She's such a sweet-heart." Miss Erma smiled then pulled out some pots and pans and placed them on the stove. "Your father said he was in the mood for some meatloaf. I think he's missing your mother. He always wants meatloaf when he's missing her."

"Sounds good to me. I guess I'll go watch the Young and The Restless with Daddy." I rolled my eyes and giggled. I hated soap operas but I sucked it up for my father.

Miss Erma took the ground beef out of the refrigerator and giggled. She knew how I felt about the television situation. "I can fix you a drink to help the time pass."

"This early?"

"Sweetie, it's 5:00 somewhere." Miss Erma winked at me.

Miss Erma had been with the family for years. She was a short, feisty, robust woman who could definitely handle my father. I adored my daddy but he was beyond stubborn. I guess that's where I get it from.

I went back into the living room to join my dad who was already enthralled in his show. I listened to him curse everybody out for being stupid which I found hilarious. I tried to pay attention but once I cuddled up on the couch with the chenille throw, I knew it was about to be lights out for me.

"Baby girl! Wake up! You've been sleep for hours!"

Daddy's voice was so commanding, he never had to call me twice. I rubbed my eyes and sat up. "What is it, Daddy?"

"Your phone has been going off nonstop. I just got off the phone with Luca. He was trying to reach you and feared the worst but I assured him you were fine. Just knocked out on my couch snoring." he chuckled.

"You know good and well that I don't snore." I laughed, tossing one of the throw pillows from the couch at him.

"I wish you did snore, maybe it would've

drowned out your phone ringing back to back."

"Sorry, Daddy." I looked at my phone and checked my missed calls, texts and voicemail before going over some details with my dad for the meeting tonight. Even though this wasn't an official business gathering, I prided myself on always being prepared.

I stood in front of the Omni Learner mirror, scrutinizing my attire for tonight's meeting. I did a 360-turn admiring my bold red Dolce & Gabbana suit. The satiny peak lapels and pockets reinforced the classic tuxedo styling of the two-button blazer tailored from stretch wool crepe. Parallel darts nipped the waist, emphasizing my curvy hips giving the menswear inspired design a more feminine silhouette. The sleeveless silk camisole paired with a ruby diamond necklace and matching earrings had me looking like I owned a Fortune 500 conglomerate. I had my hair swept up to showcase not only my jewelry but the outline of my slender neck. I was dressed to get the upmost respect which I demanded at all times. I had to, especially since my line of work required me to deal with egotistical men on a daily basis.

On the way out, I stopped to grab my briefcase. That's when daddy informed me Big Mike was coming to basically be my chaperone. I rolled my eyes. It aggravated me how daddy trusted my business judgment but he always sent one of his goons with me like I couldn't protect myself. Hell, I had a better shot than any man in the room.

Big Mike and I arrived early to the meeting. I wanted to pay my respects to the family. The atmosphere was a somber one and I hugged everyone that was in attendance. I noticed they seemed to be more in shock then grief.

I felt a hand on my back and I knew who it was before I turned around and looked. "Luca." I cracked a semi smile and stood up to hug him.

"Take a walk with me." Luca whispered in my ear. I followed him out the room.

"I need some air." Luca opened the door that led onto the balcony.

"How's your father holding up?"

"He's broken on the inside but you know my father, he keeps his feelings close to the vest."

"Sounds like someone else I know." I eyed Luca, running my hand down his arm.

"Touché." Luca tilted his head and gave me that look. You know the look men give when they're imagining your lips all over them, or recalling what it felt like being lost inside of you, well that's the look he was giving me.

"Simmer down," I remarked. "We agreed, those days are over." I reminded Luca. Plus, this wasn't the time nor the place for sex to be consuming his thoughts. We had more important issues to think about. But he was an easy temptation, especially dressed in a black tailored suit, which was in stark contrast to his olive complexion. Luca's sharp features, deep set dark brown eyes and his facial hair was always neatly trimmed perfectly around his lips.

I guess he could sense my desire for him because Luca stepped closer. He was now invading my personal space by leaning forward to kiss me.

"Don't even think about it," I scoffed.

"But I need you right now." Playing the sympathy card wasn't working for him.

"I'm right here, Luca but that's as far as it goes. You know what we had has flat lined. I don't play the side chick role very well."

"You know you miss me." Luca nudged closer to me.

"I won't lie, I miss you. But I have no intentions of letting you in my bed, ever again. I can promise you that. So, keep it cute and focus on your wife." It didn't matter what nationality, I realized that most men just ain't shit when it came to having dick control.

Luca threw his hands up to surrender. He realized this was one conversation he wasn't going to win. We then were both silent as we watched the different cars pull up.

"My father is going to be out for blood." Luca sighed. He pulled out a pack of cigarettes, lighting one up.

"You predicting a long night?" I cut my eyes over at him.

"I'm predicting something. What that is, I'm not sure. Is that Cross?" Luca squinted his eyes to focus.

My heartbeat quickened as I looked on. Sure enough, right behind Curtis Sr. was Cross.

"Croccifixio!" Luca clapped his hands together. Let's go. "Tonight, definitely just got interesting."

"What is that supposed to mean?" I hissed with a bit of attitude.

"Croccifixio is here with his father and not Curtis Jr., you don't find that odd? That can only mean one thing. Cross is taking over," Luca rationalized.

"We'll see," I countered.

"That we shall. Let's get a drink first." Luca led me to the bar and poured us both a Hennessey on the rocks. Then we took our seats at the table and waited on everyone to arrive.

Two by two the family heads marched in. I hated these meetings because I didn't trust now muthafucka here. Not even Luca. That was one of the reasons I was glad to put an end to things romantically because some good dick can cloud your judgement.

There were seven families seated at the table. And only three people were black. I used to tell my father the Italians were always waiting for us to fuck up, so they could justify slitting our throats without guilt. Daddy would tell me not to talk like that but he knew my assessment was accurate. At any moment, the same Italians who broke bread with us at the table and called us family, could quickly become our enemy.

When Cross walked in, our eyes locked for a moment. Everyone then rose from their seats to hug him like he was some great leader. I found it amusing yet infuriating. My irritation continued when the room began to fill with smoke, all because of everyone's obsession with puffing on those damn cigars. Secretly I was hoping someone would choke and drop dead right there at the table. I found myself laughing out loud at the thought.

"What's so funny?" Cross asked.

I looked up and was surprised he was speaking to me in the open but when I glanced over at his father Curtis, I saw he was enthralled in a deep conversation in the corner.

"Nothing." I kept my reply concise, then returned to my resting bitch face.

"Still mean as hell." Cross shook his head.

"Who's mean as hell? Not Charly." Luca leaned over kissing me on the cheek.

If looks could kill Luca would be in the morgue. He knew better than that. It was obvious he did that shit on purpose. But I gave him a pass since his brother was just murdered.

Luca noticed the mean mug on my face. "Maybe she is meanie." He joked.

"I'm here for business, nothing more nothing less, understood?" I stated.

"Understood." Luca nodded. He couldn't get away from me fast enough. I checked my watch wishing Francesco would hurry up.

"You got somewhere to be?" Cross remarked.

"Maybe."

"I'm aware you know how to speak in complete sentences because I just heard you do it."

"What do you want, Cross?" the moment I asked that, Francesco entered the room with his two other sons Antonio and Giovanni.

"Charly, it's good to see you love." Francesco greeted me.

I got up from my seat and hugged him. "My father sends his condolences. If he could be here he would."

"Thank you but I would rather look at you any day over your father." Francesco followed up with one of his jovial laughs.

"Behave now!" I wagged my finger at him.

"I promise." He winked before turning his attention to Cross. "Croccifixio! I heard you were back. The chosen son returns." Francesco grabbed Cross's face and kissed him on both cheeks.

I had to refrain from rolling my eyes watching the two hug and chop it up since I didn't want to bring any negative attention my way.

"Ok let's get down to business." Francesco made it clear that whomever was behind the killing of his son would be dealt with and security needed to be on point because each of us was vulnerable.

Curtis Payne then announced that Cross would be taking over the operations while he tended to his wife. He assured everyone the transition would go smoothly because Cross had to get his approval on all business dealings.

To no one's surprise, Francesco wanted to know if anyone had business to handle with him. Of course, I was ready and prepared. I slid over his envelope and he thanked me. Family death or not, this man way always about his bottom line and that was money. I believe it was the only thing a man like Francesco would ever truly mourn for.

After the meeting, Francesco asked to speak to Cross and I privately. "I wanted to talk to you both. I know there's no love lost between your families," Francesco stated, getting straight to the point. "I would hope that you two can set aside any animosity and work together so your families can move forward. There was a time, your father's loved each other like brothers. Call an old man sentimental but no matter how ancient I feel, I never stop thinking, life is too short and death is too final. Once you meet your maker, there is no time to get over unresolved issues. The two of you remember that." Francesco gave a stern glare while pointing his finger at us. Then he spoke directly to Cross. "I'm glad you're home, Cross and I will light a candle for your mother and my beloved niece."

"Thank you, Sir." His tone was confident and strong but when the anguish set in, Cross couldn't hide the sorrow in his eyes regarding his mother.

"We will do our best to work things out," I stepped forward and said wanting to shift this cloud of sadness that was now lurking over us.

"I knew you wouldn't disappoint, Charly. I'll leave you two to talk for a moment. Join us when you're done." Francesco left us alone in the room.

There was this awkward silence between

us once left alone. We were trying not to stare each other down but there was this undeniable chemistry we shared. Being so close was stirring up old feelings that I wanted to keep deeply buried. Unfortunately, my mind drifted back to the last time we were alone and how Cross was knee deep inside of me making love. All these years later, no man had been able to give my body such pleasure, not even Luca. I tried not to let my mind wonder how crazy, Cross sex game must be now.

"Is your mother sick?" I asked, wanting to get my mind out the sex gutter.

"Yeah, she has early onset of Alzheimer's."

"I'm sorry. Miss Lita is such a sweet lady."

"Yeah, she's pretty amazing. But umm, I don't want to talk about my mother right now if you don't mind." The gloom in Cross's eyes made them appear darker than usual, if possible.

"I understand. Let's get back to business. Our fathers are the definition of stubborn, so bringing about this family unity Francesco is hoping for won't be easy."

Cross made a face that made me chuckle. "You're right about that. Where is Charlie by the way?"

"He broke his leg. The healing process has been slow, so I've been running things."

"I see. Look at you," he smirked. Cross stared down at my five-inch pointed heels and worked his way up to the subtle yet sexy cleavage, compliments of my silk camisole. "I'm impressed. You have beauty, brains and some gangsta wit' you. Don't know why I'm surprised by the gangsta part since you were raised by Charlie," he laughed. "But seriously, you're the full package." Cross gave me a lustful gaze.

"Stop looking at me like that."

"Like what? Can't a man admire a woman's beauty or does this particular man, make you nervous?" Cross moved closer to me. My eyes slightly closed feeling seduced by the fresh, sensual yet masculine scent of his cologne. It was potent...making Cross almost impossible to resist.

"Nervous? Never that!" I said defiantly.

"Good, the last thing I want to do is make you nervous." Cross stepped even closer and every inch of my body had become weak. I was beginning to think the man was wearing kryptonite disguised as cologne.

"So, what do you want?" I stepped back

needing to put some space between us. I refused to look directly at Cross. Between his alluring scent and hypnotic eyes, I was about to be standing in front of him naked wearing nothing but my stilettos.

"Is that a trick question?"

"Do I look like a trick?"

"Why are you so damn mean? Can't we just have a nice conversation? Hey I missed you. Oh, I missed you too. Let's do lunch and catch up. You know regular shit people say to each other." The sarcasm Cross gave me was real.

"Are you done with your version of how our conversation should go?" I folded my arms and stared him down.

Cross closed in on the gap between us. Personal space be damned. He lifted my face and leaned down to kiss me.

Don't kiss him, you better not kiss him back. Stay strong, but damn his lips are soft. I could feel myself weakening and just as I started to give in to temptation Luca opened the door and Cross stepped back.

"I hope I'm not interrupting but my father wants you to join us." Luca shot me an intense stare letting me know he was pissed.

"We're just finishing up here anyway." Cross told him.

"Actually, we're done. Here I come," I said to Luca but Cross grabbed my arm before I could walk away.

"I need to get your number so we can set up a meeting."

I jerked my arm away and pulled a business card out of my briefcase and handed it to him. He in return handed me his.

"I'll call you tomorrow," Cross stated without taking his eyes off me.

Luca stood at the door and waited for me. "What was that about?" he questioned as we walked out together.

"It's nothing."

I spent another hour or so mingling before I was ready to leave. Normally, I would welcome the attention from two extremely good looking men but having both Cross and Luca keeping an eye on me was uncomfortable. I felt like every move I made in the room was being scrutinized by them.

It seemed everyone had the same idea because when I made my exit they all followed. As we walked out to our awaiting cars, I was in

Charly's world, debating with myself, if it was a mistake I hesitated in kissing Cross back. Before I could decide, pandemonium broke out. Shots filled the air catching all of us off guard. Big Mike jumped on top of me covering me with his huge body. My driver, George was able to get the door open and they both got me inside.

"Drive!" Big Mike hollered.

It was complete chaos as numerous cars were speeding away simultaneously trying to escape the hail of bullets raining down.

"This has got to be an inside job. How the hell did they get past all that security?" I fussed. "George, did you see anything?"

"Nothing unusual but there were a lot of people coming and going. I guess to pay their respects. But I'm with you, this was an inside job."

My phone started vibrating. It was an unknown number so I didn't answer and let it go to voicemail. Once they left a message, I checked and realized the unknown caller was Cross. He was out of breath and speaking low, but he wanted to make sure I was straight.

Not wanting to appear too eager to hear his voice, I opted to send him a text instead of placing a call.

I'm Ok, you?
We good. I'll call you later.

In a split second my mind went from Cross to my dad. I was positive he was waiting up for me and we had a lot to discuss.

Daddy, Big Mike, George and I sat up talking about everything that happened tonight. Daddy being a stickler for details, wanted each of our point of view on what we saw, heard and even felt.

"You have to rely on all of your senses. One may pick up something the other didn't. And most people never listen to their intuition which screams the loudest, unless you keep ignoring it. Then the voice begins to fade away." Daddy reminded us.

I waited until after George and Big Mike retired to their quarters so I could speak to my dad in private. He needed to know what Francesco wanted.

"Daddy, can I come in?"

"Yeah, baby girl."

My father seemed comfortable in his bed

watching TV and I didn't want to upset him but this couldn't wait. I sat on the edge of the bed. "When we were talking earlier, I left out something. Francesco asked to speak to me and Cross alone. He wants us to work together to bring peace between you and Curtis."

"Ugh not again! Why won't he leave this alone?"

"I don't know maybe because Miss Lita is ill."

"Ill?" A look of concern came across my father's face.

"Yeah, Cross said she has early onset Alzheimer's."

"Damn! I'm sorry to hear that about Lita but it changes nothing when it comes to my feelings towards Curtis."

"I get that but Francesco is adamant the two of you come together. We both know how pushy Francesco is when he wants something. Then again, we always have the option of getting out the business. We've made more than enough money and most of our businesses are legit now. With you being sick, no one would blame you for walking away."

"That's easier said than done, Charly. Everything I do is for you and Cadence. When it's time to get out, we'll get out."

"I know and we appreciate it." I could see this conversation wasn't going anywhere. "I'm exhausted, I'ma take a hot bath and read a little to clear my head. Good night." I kissed my father on his cheek and headed out.

"Goodnight, baby girl."

The bubble bath did wonders for my body. It seemed to wash away the remnants of tonight's stress. I was good and relaxed as I climbed into my bed. Forget Italian spun Egyptian cotton sateen, I like my t-shirt sheets and Miss Erma remembered. I snuggled under my soft blanket and pulled my comforter up to my chin and as soon as I drifted off to sleep my phone went off.

"Hello?"

"What up, Charly it's me Cross. Were you sleeping?"

"I just laid down."

"Oh, I wanted to confirm our meeting tomorrow."

"There's not another lockdown?"

"Not that I know of but you would think as crazy as tonight was. Man, I did not miss this shit."

"It must've been a nice existence living in peace. What brought you back into the lion's den?"

"My Pops did but you know how that is."

"Pretty much," I said, thinking about the discussion I had with my dad less than an hour ago.

"I meant what I said though. I did miss you."

"Whatever, Cross." I rolled my eyes while listening to him.

"I'm serious."

"Well you showed it, didn't you? I enjoyed all the letters and phone calls over the years." I was laying the sarcasm on thick.

"You know things were complicated back then."

"What's changed? Things are still complicated." I sat up in my bed, quickly becoming way too invested into this conversation.

"For one, I'm a grown man now and I don't do anything I don't want to."

I sucked my teeth. "Yeah okay."

"I showed you tonight when I kissed you.

Even though at first you acted like you didn't wanna kiss me back. Right when I was making headway, Luca's ass interrupted us."

I didn't respond. I just listened trying to come up with a slick comeback.

"But it was still nice. Like I said, I missed you," Cross insisted.

"I'm getting sleepy," I lied. Listening to Cross's voice had me wide awake. But I realized I needed to get off the phone before I said something to him that I would later regret. "What time are we meeting tomorrow and where?" I needed to change the subject and wrap this conversation up.

"How about Gibson's Bar and Steakhouse at 1:00?"

"Ok, see you then."

"Rest easy, Charly mean lady Brinx."

"You too Cross corny as hell Payne." Cross's laugh echoed through the phone as I ended the call.

I hung up wondering why his voice had to sound so sexy. Even his laugh was sexy. I tossed and turned until I eventually fell asleep dreaming about the day I would feel Cross Payne inside of me again.

Chapter 4

Cross

I got up early to meet with the realtor to check out the penthouse at the luxury building downtown. The moment I stepped into the open, spacious unit, I decided it had to be mine. There was more than enough room for me and my kids. So, I bought it straight out with cash which got me what some call a liquidity discount for being able to close quickly. Money will always open the door and the more you're willing to toss out, the wider it opens.

With my new purchase, came nonstop visits to an exclusive furniture store my realtor recommended, that luckily had all the essentials I needed. Once I got fixated on something, my mind would keep going until it was done to my liking. Due to that fact, not only did I pay a crazy amount of dough for the furniture I bought, but I paid even extra because I wanted my shit delivered asap. It all worked out lovely and I was pleased with my new place so my mind was at ease. Once I got my home situation in order, I could focus all my attention on business and if I played my cards right, Charly would be an added bonus.

I checked the time and hightailed it to Star-bucks. I was excited about our dinner date at Eddie V's but I couldn't wait until then to see Charly again.

I walked into Starbucks and there she was looking beautiful as ever. I stared at her lips as she licked them. She glanced up, noticing me and nodded her head without cracking a smile.

"I can't get a smile?" I questioned walking up to her. *Damn, she's gorgeous. The one that got away*, I thought to myself.

"No." Charly snapped.

"Mean ass!" I walked over to the counter to order an espresso. I sat down across from Charly while waiting for them to call my name.

"Did I say I wanted company?" Charly asked with a slight attitude.

"No but I didn't think you would mind. Especially since the kiss we shared last night." That kiss kept me up most of the night as if her lips were calling me but I decided to keep that part to myself.

Charly slightly shifted her body in the chair and grunted. "Oh that."

"Yeah that. I think you owe me a repeat since your boy interrupted us."

"Have you lost your mind?" Charly fussed raising her voice.

As much as I got a kick out of messing with Charly, she looked like she was ready to reach across the table to slap me. "Calm down. You too pretty to be so mean. I'm messing with you. We used to be able to laugh together, what happened?"

Charly looked me dead in my eyes and said, "You left!"

Charly had this fire in her eyes I'd never seen before. I swear she was burning a hole through me. "I didn't have a choice you gotta believe me."

"Cross!" The barista called my name and I got up to get my order. I debated on whether to leave or not. *Fuck it, we need to talk.* "I think we need to clear the air but not here. Can we talk in my truck?"

"It's not that serious, it's all good."

"I don't think it is. We should talk. How can we get our fathers to squash they beef, if we have unresolved issues?"

"A'ight," Charly agreed but I could hear the disdain in her voice.

I waited for Charly to gather her belongings, so we could walk out together. "I'm parked right here," I said, opening the door for her.

Once inside I pleaded my case. I turned in my seat to face her. "Can you look at me for a second, I want to see your eyes?" to my surprise she obliged without giving me any lip.

"Charly, I'm sorry. You know how I felt about you but I was still young and I had to do what my father wanted. That's why I left you a letter explaining everything. But you never responded."

"Letter what letter? I never got any letter."

"What? I left you a letter with my brother Santi. He swore he gave it to you."

"He lied. I never got a letter from you." The sadness in Charly's eyes told me she was telling the truth.

I became consumed with rage and wanted to pounce my fist through the glass windshield. "All this time I figured you regretted what happened between us and wanted to put the night we spent together behind you. I don't understand why Santi would lie to me. I told him to bring you the letter personally."

"Well he didn't!" Charly retorted.

I shook my head in disgust and my breathing increased. "I can't believe he would do that. But why?" I asked out loud as if Charly could give me the answer. The only person who could, was Santi and he better had a good fuckin' reason.

"Wow! I don't know what to say Cross. I was so infuriated at you for just disappearing on me and then," Charly's words faded and her bottom lip began to tremble before continuing. "Then, I found out you were getting married." She turned to me and locked her eyes deep into mine, as if Charly wanted what she was about to say next to resonate profoundly in my soul. "It broke my heart. I had two choices. I could either let myself fall into a deep depression or suck it up and move on with my life." Charly's voice went in and out as she spoke to me, like he was trying to fight back tears.

"All this time, I thought you didn't want anything to do wit' me and you were thinking I left you and never looked back. Charly, please forgive me. I figured you didn't think I was worth the bullshit we'd have to go through in order to be together. I knew our fathers wouldn't understand but it didn't matter to me. I had a plan all worked out in my head. I wanted us to run off somewhere, anywhere, as long as we were together. I waited and waited for weeks to hear back from you. When I didn't, I decided to do me. I went a lil' wild and I'll admit, that's how I ended up with my wife but it was supposed to be you. It was always supposed to be you."

"This is all too much." Charly leaned her head against the passenger door. "That one night changed my life forever. You have no idea."

Seeing Charly in so much pain enraged me even more. My phone went off and when I answered it was the store letting me know they were on their way with my furniture delivery. I turned on the ignition and pulled off.

"Where are we going?" Charly glanced over at me like I was the enemy.

I didn't answer I just continued to drive until I pulled up to my new spot.

"Nigga, what you doing?!"

"Just come on!" I huffed.

"For what?" Charly sucked her teeth and folded her arms as if she was determined to give me a hard fuckin' time.

"Damn Charly! Can you just bring yo' ass on!" I saw her hesitate for a few seconds before finally getting out the car and following me.

As we walked through the lobby I could see the furniture company unloading. That gave me just a few minutes to show Charly my new spot.

"I wanted you to be the first person to see my new place." I told her as we entered. "Let me show you around," I smiled, wanting to break down the wall Carly had put up between us.

"This is super nice and spacious. This building is hard to get into. Really exclusive. I heard there's a waiting list. Impressive," Charly nodded looking around.

"It could probably use a woman's touch. What you think?" I was testing the waters but she wasn't ready to bite.

"I guess you better go find that woman to give you the touch you lookin' for." Charly started to laugh and I couldn't help but smile. She was trying to meet me half way and I was here for it. I wanted to kiss her but the doorbell rang.

It was the delivery men from the furniture store. After I showed them where everything was supposed to go, they did their thing, I tipped them, thanked them and they were out. Everything went smoothly and I was now able to direct my attention on who mattered most to me right now. Charly was sitting on the sectional and seemed to be in deep thought.

"You okay?" I asked, sitting down next to her.

"I'm just thinking."

"About what? Am I keeping you from something or someone?"

"No that's not it. I'm processing everything that you told me earlier. I don't live in what ifs but I would be lying if it didn't cross my mind."

"I feel you. I hope you believe me now, when I say I missed you."

"I missed you too." Charly cut her eyes over at me.

"Now see, did that kill you to admit?" I teased.

"I think it did kill me just a little bit," Charly giggled, putting her pointer and thumb fingers together.

"I love seeing you smile."

"Yo, you so corny!" Charly shook her head but I caught a slight grin creep across her face.

"Man, you so hard on a nigga!" I laughed. I didn't mind since she was letting her guard down a little.

"Stop looking at me like that."

"What I do? We're sitting here having a conversation. I have to look at you."

"Not like that."

"Not like what...like I want you because you know I do."

"Is that right?" Charly seemed completely unfazed by the words coming out my mouth so I went in for the win. I grabbed her by the back of the neck and pulled her close to me. I kissed her and kissed her hard too. I wanted her to know that I meant that shit.

Before I knew it I felt her body relax and she kissed me back. Our tongues explored each other's mouths and when I heard a slight moan escape her lips. I knew I had her right where I wanted.

Chapter 5

Charly

The way Cross grabbed me, was a turn on. He had this aggressive streak he unleashed, when determined to get what he wanted. That's how we wound up in bed the first time and ended up going half on a baby. We exchanged passionate kisses until needing a moment to breathe. His hands roamed my body and as he started to undress me, I gave no resistance. Cross bit into my neck then eased the intoxicating pain by licking his tongue down my shoulder.

Damn I know he doesn't remember that's my spot. I closed my eyes and let him do his thing. He stripped me down and when I opened my eyes he was already naked too. We both had lust in our eyes. His body was even more sculpted and delectable than I remembered.

When he laid me down on the plush carpet and hovered over me, Cross's aggressive touch turned gentle and methodical. He took his time sprinkling kisses all over me as if wanting to become reacquainted with my body. His tongue gave my nipples a warm sensation as he caressed my breasts before working his way down to my stomach. My body began to tingle with anticipation. Cross ran his wet tongue up and down my inner thighs before it made love to my clit. But once he replaced his tongue with his thick dick, I completely lost it. He mounted me and entered slowly but with the length and girth he was working with, it didn't matter. I screamed out his name, burying my nails deep into his skin. His strokes were slow yet steady until he was completely engulfed inside of me.

Cross moaned my name and then life changed in that moment. I met him thrust for thrust and each time Cross professed his love for me I told him back. What the hell was really going on? I'm not a talker but for some reason I couldn't keep my mouth shut. My insides were thirsty for him. He flipped me over and I was more than ready to show him I could hold my own but that man fucked me into submission. Even once I got on top, Cross was in control. I didn't mind because once my legs started shaking and we both climaxed, everything at that moment felt perfect.

"Charly, I love you," Cross said before collapsing on me. I ran my fingers thru his hair, kissed his head and told him I loved him too. I instantly regretted my confession, the moment the words left my mouth.

I woke up to kisses on my neck. For a second I had to remember where I was because the ceiling didn't look familiar at all.

"Hey, baby!" Cross said sitting on the plush rug we christened.

"Hi." I sat up and wiped my eyes. "How long have I been out?"

"It's after 3. I didn't wanna wake you so I called myself putting some things away, I purchased earlier. I don't know about you but I'm starving." Cross's eyes glanced down at my naked body.

"Don't even think about it," I said, pulling the cashmere blanket closer to my body. "I need to get in the shower." As I was getting up, I heard my phone going off. "Can you hand me my phone?" Cross obliged. I checked my text messages and voice mails. I had been MIA for hours and people were getting worried. The first return call I made was to my daughter Cadence.

"Ma, where you been? I've been calling you all day!"

"I'm so sorry. I got tied up. Is everything okay?"

"Everything is fine. I was just worried. It's not like you to go missing."

"Awww, you were worried about me. That's so sweet. I missed you too."

"Blah, blah, blah. I didn't say all that, Ma! Can I go to a party this weekend?" she jumped to the next subject.

"What party, Cadence?" I rolled my eyes, thinking how she's always going somewhere.

"It's at Diamond's house."

"You and Diamond are gonna be the death of me," I sighed. "I guess but I will be calling Jackie to confirm."

"Thanks! Miss Jackie is gonna be there. I'll bring you home a plate."

"Don't try to bribe me because you know I love Jackie's cooking. But yeah do that, bring me a plate...a big plate," I laughed.

"One more thing. Can we go pick out something super cute for me to wear to the party? I saw these shoes at Auntie Tia's store that I love but I need the perfect outfit for it."

"Yeah we can go shopping tomorrow after you get out of school."

"There's no school tomorrow, it's a teacher's workday."

"Oh that's right. Then we'll go tomorrow around noon. Don't be late for work today either."

"I won't, Ma!"

"A'ight. Love you."

"Love you more!"

I was so caught up in my conversation with Cadence, I'd forgotten I wasn't alone until I looked over and noticed Cross. He was staring at me with a smile spread across his face.

"What's with the smile?"

"I was just watching you doing your mommy thing. It's cute."

I raised an eyebrow and tilted my head. "What's so cute about it?"

"I like seeing you in your element...a softer side." Cross leaned back against the sofa. "So, tell me about your daughter."

I instantly got a lump in my throat. I started to sweat and I couldn't think about anything except for how much Cadence favored Cross. I always thought she looked like me minus the eyes but staring at this man, I see my daughter all in his face.

I stood up. "There's not much to tell, she's a typical teenager. She's my world though."

"Yeah, tell me about it, I have three. 16, 15, and 13. One girl and two boys."

"Oh, that's nice. I need to get in the shower," I remarked, cutting the conversation short before he could start asking me more questions. It was one thing, keeping my secret about Cadence when I believed Cross had abandoned me but now that I knew the truth, it complicated things. Making love to him, saying I love you, yet not revealing we shared a beautiful daughter together, had me feeling like a complete fraud. If our relationship continued, it would only be a matter of time before everything blew up in my face. I had to do whatever necessary to stop that from happening.

Chapter 6

Cross

"I'm glad you agreed to have dinner with me. You seemed anxious to get away after you took your shower," I said to Charly, thinking how beautiful she looked sitting across the table from me.

"You didn't leave me much of a choice. You wouldn't take me back to my car unless I said yes."

"So, I played hardball. Are you mad?"

"Not at all." Charly beamed.

"You really are incredibly beautiful when you smile and with your hair curly like that. Why don't you wear it curly more often?" In its natural curly state, she reminded me of the Charly I left behind.

"Thank you but I got it wet in the shower. It's the only reason I'm wearing it, in its natural state. I prefer it straight."

"You look beautiful either way but with it curly like that," I said reaching over to stroke her hair. "It reminds me of the Charly I made love to for the first time all those years ago."

"I'm not that Charly anymore. The sweet and innocent girl you left behind."

"I explained all that to you. After the incredible sex we had last night, I thought we were past the bullshit." Before Charly could respond, the waitress brought our food. I decided to table the discussion until after I devoured my porterhouse steak and Charly ate her ribeye. We dug into our food and there was complete silence at the table. It wasn't until we both cleaned our plates, did I try to engage in conversation again.

"Like I was saying before, I thought everything was cool between us. Was I wrong?" I questioned, taking a swig of my Hennessey.

"It is...but." Charly paused and her face became serious.

"But what...are you wondering where do we go from here? My Pops and your father still hate each other so where does that leave us?"

"I'm trying not to think about it. Today hasn't been about them and everything is good. We're out in public and not once did either of us say I hope no one sees us together."

"Valid point. It hasn't crossed my mind. But if not today, eventually someone will see us together. Honestly I don't care. We're grown now and our parents can't dictate who we want to be with. I let you get away once, I won't make that mistake again."

"Really?" Charly didn't sound convinced.

"I'm serious, babe. Don't get me wrong, I love my kids but you should have been their mother and your daughter should've been mine. Where's her daddy at anyway?"

Charly spit out her merlot and started to cough. I got up out of my seat to make sure she was ok.

"I'm fine," she said between coughs. "It just went down the wrong way." Charly wiped her mouth with her napkin. She composed herself and looked at me strangely. "What were you saying?"

"I was asking about your daughter's father. Cadence right?"

"Yeah, I don't really like to talk about him."

"Is he that bad?"

"More like out of sight out of mind. But we're good, Cadence is taken care of."

"No doubt but I was just wondering. My ex-wife is something special and unfortunately I don't mean that in no positive way. We tried to make it work but the longer we stayed the more miserable we both became. I'm surprised you never married."

"Hmmm! I hadn't met my equal." Charly managed to swallow her merlot without choking this time.

"That's because you're looking at him."

"You were never short on confidence but I hear you talking," Charly scoffed.

I reached across the table and held her hand. "I want us to be together. Is that what you want?"

Charly was quiet for a moment. "It sounds idyllic, it would be pretty perfect actually if it wasn't so complicated," she admitted, unable to conceal the concern on her face.

"I'm willing to fight for you but I gotta know, are you willing to fight for me? You're all your father has, so I can't see him disowning you but my dad has two other sons to replace me with."

"You would walk away from your family for me?"

"Yes but only if you're willing to do the same because I can't fight this battle alone. I can see the wheels turning in your head. What you thinking?"

"I can't let you walk out of your mother's life. She needs you."

"That's true she does but she wouldn't want me to be unhappy either." I reached out and rubbed Charly's hands.

"I want to be with you, I do," Charly said, with sincerity.

"Then what's holding you back?"

"It's more than just us to consider. I have a daughter, you have three kids. I'm not saying we should stay away from each other but we should proceed with caution. There could be a lot of collateral damage."

"I understand. We'll take it day by day. If nobody ask, we don't tell. If and when people do find out, we'll deal with it then. Let's make this about us not them because I'm not letting you go ever again."

"I agree, it's about us."

"My penthouse can be our spot. Our little get away. We have something special and we can't let nobody destroy that because I love you, Charly Brinks."

"And I love you, Cross Payne."

"There you go with that crazy look on yo' face again. What's up wit' you? Are you not ready for this? If not speak up now."

"It's not that. I'm all in. But I need you to understand, this is new to me. I'm usually in control of my feelings and with you it's different, it's always been different. That's why it hurt me to the core when you disappeared out my life. Since then I put a wall up with men. They became a means to an end and I reserved my love for those closest to me. Then you show up and now all these emotions I've never felt before, along with buried feeling, hit me all at once. I was taught emotions can get you killed in our line of work. We have to stay numb to the game in order to survive it. So this is gonna take a little adjustment on my part."

"I hear you and I understand where you coming from but emotions are a necessity in a relationship. We gotta separate the two. I need all of you, if I'm giving you all of me. We gotta be in this together, Charly, or not at all."

"Baby, I got you. I'm all in," Charly promised stroking my hand.

I stared into Charly's eyes and I could see the love but there was also hesitation. I even sensed fear. My initial thought, was Charly being afraid of her father finding out about us but my gut was telling me it ran much deeper. Whatever it was, only time would tell.

Chapter 7

Charly

After being up under Cross for the last few days, it was a relief to be sleeping in my own bed. It wasn't that I didn't enjoy having Cross inside me but that man was a stallion. He wore me out. The much needed sleep was so damn good, it felt as if my body was resting on a cloud but the peaceful feeling didn't last long. With my eyes closed I could feel someone in the room with me. I was laying on my side so I slowly slid my hand under my pillow and pulled out my nine. I rolled over and aimed.

"Damn, bitch you gonna shoot me?" Tia screamed, turning on the light.

"Girl, don't play wit' yo' life like that. What you doing here?" I asked sitting up in the bed. "I'm relieved it's you but I almost shot my best friend."

"I see!" Tia leaned her head back looking shocked. "Now can you please put that gun away. You didn't show up for lunch so I came to check on you." Tia plopped down on the bed, still eyeing the gun in my hand.

"Girl, I got so much to tell you," I said, putting my nine back under the pillow.

"I'm all ears. So what's going on with the lockdown?"

"I'll get to the lockdown situation in a minute, first let me tell you about Cross." As I filled Tia in on everything, she sat with her mouth wide open. I took my hand pushed her chin up. "Say something fool!"

"Honey, I'm in my feelings! On one hand, OMG Cross didn't leave you. He wanted to be with you just like you wanted to be with him. Your life would have been so different. We need to fuck Santi up but then again everything happens for a reason and girl you got the afterglow going on big time. I'm happy for you. Cross is your one true love but what about Cadence? You gotta tell him about her and then what about your dad? Girl, this is a lot," Tia shook her head.

"Ya think? I don't know what to do."

"You always know what to do."

"Not with this one. Do I just casually say, oh by the way Cross, we have a daughter?"

"Sounds about right to me."

I was going to clown Tia but my phone started ringing. "I don't recognize this number," I said, debating whether to answer.

"Girl, answer the phone. You act like you hiding from bill collectors."

"Damn, they calling back. Let me answer." After saying hello my mind sort of froze and then I dropped my phone. "I gotta go!" I screamed, jumping out the bed.

"Charly, what's going on? You're scaring me."

"Cadence is in the hospital." I ran into my closet and pulled out a sweat suit to throw on.

"What happened?"

"I don't know, Tia! All I heard was surgery

and I needed to get to the hospital!" I screamed as I got dressed and put my sneakers on.

"I'll drive. I got your purse and your phone."

I ran down the stairs with Tia on my heels. Luckily there was no police in sight because Tia was flying. She cut a thirty minute drive in half. We arrived to North Western hospital in no time. We rushed to the receptionist.

"My daughter Cadence Brinx was brought in," I said breathing heavy.

The lady looked in the computer. "Yes, if you'll have a seat in this room over there, the doctor will be with you shortly."

"Is that all you can tell me? Was she in an accident? What happened?" I needed answers before I lost my mind.

"She was brought in unconscious and bleeding."

"Bleeding? Bleeding from what...where? That's not telling me nothing!" I screamed at the lady.

"Ma'am, I'll let the doctor know that you're here. Just have a seat please."

"This some bullshit!" I barked, ready to pick up one of these chairs and toss it at the re-ceptionist. "And where the hell is Diamond?" I stormed off in the direction of the waiting area.

"Give me your phone, I'll call her." Tia walked over to the corner.

I could hear her cursing but I couldn't process anything. "Lord please let my baby be ok," I mumbled over and over again.

"She's on her way. That fool was still in the mall looking for her. She said they split up then she couldn't find her and had been calling but didn't get an answer."

"I have to call my dad," I said, putting Diamond in the back of my mind. Of course my father answered right away and I told him everything I knew. He wanted to come but he didn't need to be up here with all these germs. I promised to call him as soon as I learned anything.

"We're going to think positive. Cadence will be fine." Tia tried to calm my nerves but that wouldn't happen until the doctor told me what was wrong with my baby girl.

Minutes turned into an hour until finally I got some answers. "Ms. Brinx?" the doctor came out.

"Yes, how is my daughter?" I ran up on the doctor so fast, I almost knocked him down.

"Her appendix ruptured, so we had to operate to remove it. The operation went fine and she's resting comfortably."

"Her appendix?" I was beyond confused. Cadence never had an issue with her appendix.

"Thank God she's ok." Tia said, putting her arm around me.

My phone went off. Tia turned to look who was calling. "It's Diamond. I'll get it."

"Can I see her?" I asked the doctor while Tia was speaking to Diamond.

"Sure come on back. She's still out of it but your daughter will be fine."

"I'm glad to hear that. But what made her appendix rupture?"

"It's more common than you think." The doctor explained as we walked to the room.

We entered the room and my baby was resting peacefully. "Your mother's here." I kissed Cadence on the forehead and sat down next to her bed. As I asked the doctor a bunch of questions and listened to her answers, I rubbed my baby's hand. When she left us alone I prayed and thanked God. I felt helpless and as a mother that's the worst feeling in the world.

When I initially got the call that Cadence was in the hospital, all kinds of thoughts ran through my head. The first thing I assumed was maybe this was some kind of retaliation from the other night. I had to figure out a way to convince my dad it was time for us to get out the game. I couldn't live my life with this sort of stress anymore. I watched Cadence sleep just like I used to do when she was a baby. I was at peace and that's what I wanted for us, our family...peace of mind.

"Knock knock!" Tia sang, "Can I come in?" Tia said as she stood in the doorway.

"Oh girl, my bad. I didn't mean to walk off and leave you in the waiting room. I got caught up in talking to the doctor."

"No explanation needed. How's Cadence doing?"

"The doctor said she's doing good. Me on the other hand," I shook my head. "I was so scared." I started crying which I was trying to avoid.

"I know you're worried but Cadence is a fighter. She'll get through this and so will you," Tia hugged me and said. "That's your baby, of course you were scared. But she's fine. I told Diamond not to come to the hospital and just go home because Cadence wasn't awake, plus I know she irks your soul," Tia giggled.

"Thank you, girl." I wiped the tears from my eyes. "Oh, I've got to call my dad."

"I already did. I had to really talk him out of coming."

"Girl, you know how my daddy is."

"Charly!" I heard a distinctive voice call out my name.

"Cross." I said his name calmly as I stood up but that didn't stop the color draining from my face.

Cross rushed over and hugged me. "I came as soon as I heard. Is she okay?" Cross looked over my shoulder at Cadence.

"How did you know I was here?" I gave Tia a nasty look. She motioned, as if she zipped her mouth and threw her hands up like not me.

"My Pops told me. He was on the phone with Francesco when your father called. They didn't know what happened so they immediately thought it was related to the other night. As soon as my dad told me, I came straight here. So what happened?"

"Her appendix ruptured. They had to do surgery to remove it."

"Thank God she's ok. I had to get my appendix removed when I was younger. She'll be sore for a while but once she heals up, she'll be as good as new."

"Oh yeah, I remember that." I cut my eyes at Tia who had a bewildered look upon her face as well.

"I know you had to be scared. Why didn't you call me?" Cross held me close and it felt good to be in his arms.

"Ma?" Cadence mumbled.

I rushed to her side. "Baby, I'm here. I'm right here." I stroked her hair and kissed her face. Cadence stirred around trying to wake herself up.

She struggled to open her eyes due to being drugged up. "What happened? Where am I?"

I explained the situation to her but Cadence was fixated on Cross. She blinked over and over again as if to clear her vision. My heart beat quickened with each blink Cadence gave. She couldn't stop staring at the man who stood only a few feet away from her.

"Is that my father?"

"Huh?!" Fear gripped my body and I couldn't speak.

"His eyes, his eyes are just like mine. You said I had my father's eyes." Cadence looked at me for answers.

I froze, I couldn't look at Cadence, I couldn't look at Cross.

"Hey, Candy girl! They got you all pumped up on the good stuff." Tia moved me out the way. "Sis, go get you something to drink." She nodded her head towards the door.

I could see Cross examining Cadence face. My legs felt like jelly. I wanted to run but I couldn't fuckin move!

"Hey pretty lady, my name is Cross. I'm glad you're ok. How old are you?"

"Sixteen."

"Nice. When's your birthday?"

"April 11th."

"April 11th, huh?" Cross turned and looked at me with daggers in his eyes.

Chapter 8

Cross

The more I stared at Charly the angrier I became. The look on her face said it all. Cadence was my daughter. As much as I wanted to tear that hospital room apart, I couldn't let this be my daughter's first memory of me.

"I'll be back sweetie. Let me talk to your mother for a minute." I smiled at Cadence and she returned the smile. She had her mother's smile but those eyes, those were my mother's eyes...my eyes.

I grabbed Charly by the arm and pulled her into the hallway. I had never seen her scared before until now.

"Why didn't you tell me?" the wrath in me spilled out in my voice.

"Stop screaming before she hears you!" Charly snapped.

Still holding onto her arm, we walked until we found an empty waiting room. I shoved her down in the chair. I watched her demeanor change and I knew I was in for a battle. "You kept my daughter from me!"

Charly jumped up. "You muthafucka, you! I didn't keep a damn thing from you. I wasn't the one who left. I did the best I knew how to do in the situation I was in. So don't you dare stand here all self-righteous and shit like I did you wrong. Her life has been in my hands all these years. MINE!"

"I told you I sent for you!"

"And you never followed up. You never called, nothing! So how bad did you really want to be with me?"

"Are you serious right now? I was willing to walk away from my family for you!" I screamed at her.

"So you say." Charly sucked her teeth and folded her arms.

"Oh now I'm a liar? I asked you about her father yesterday. Why didn't you tell me then? Were you ever gonna tell me?"

"I didn't know how. I never expected to see you again after all of these years."

"How were we gonna build a life together with a lie? Didn't you know I would put two and two together when I laid eyes on her?"

"I was going to tell you." Charly's voice cracked.

"When...before or after we fucked again?" My words cut Charly like a knife but I didn't care at that moment. I wanted her to be enraged just like the fuck I was. "How you lay wit' a man, tell 'em you love him but keep him from his own flesh and blood? What kind of woman does that?" I could see Charly's wall going back up with each passing moment but it made me no difference because my wall was now up too.

"Go spend time with your daughter." Charly said, walking off.

I fought back the tears of anger in my eyes and gathered my thoughts. Then I went to the gift shop and bought all the flowers and stuff animals in the store. By the time I returned to Cadence room, she had fallen back to sleep. Tia was sitting there watching her.

"What did you do, buy out the entire gift shop?" Tia teased. "Let me help you out," she said taking some of the vases of flowers out of my hands and putting them on the table. "Where's Charly?" I could hear the concern in her voice.

"I don't know. We got into it," I explained, placing the rest of the flowers and gifts on the tray and the table.

"Let me speak to you for a minute." Tia walked out the room and I followed her.

"I know you may think I'm over stepping my bounds and this is none of my business but Charly is my best friend which makes it my business," Tia stated calmly. "That's your daughter laying in that bed but she's my Goddaughter too. I was there when Charly found out she was pregnant. I was there when she cried for you night after night. I was there when her father stopped speaking to her when she got pregnant. I was also there when she lied about who the father was to protect you because although she felt abandoned, she didn't want her father to harm you. It was me who was there when Cadence came into this world. This entire situation is messed up and I'm gonna tell you exactly what I'm gonna tell Charly. Right the wrong. It's that simple.

"It ain't that simple though," I cut in and said.

"That's where you wrong. Candy took one look at you and knew you were her daddy. There was no anger in her voice. Her eyes lit up. Why? Because my friend raised her right. She raised her to be a loving young lady. Do you have a right to be angry...of course. Did Charly? Yes. Both of you were robbed. There was no malice on either of your parts. Right the wrong. Whether you two decide to move forward or not, doesn't change the fact you share a beautiful daughter together, who deserves both of her parents. You and Charly, are stubborn as hell. Why are you arguing instead of accepting life and circumstances as they are? I know she loves you. I heard you love her too. So quit ego tripping and man up."

"You something else, Tia," I cracked. "That's some real shit you just spit though. Much respect," I smiled giving her a hug.

"Yeah I know, I'm that bitch." Tia laughed. "I can spit them words of wisdom when necessary.

Now go be with your daughter. You don't need to waste any more time. You all have a lot of catching up to do."

I went back in the room and sat down in the chair. Tia's words resonated with me. I tried to put myself in Charly's shoes. I didn't agree with what she did but a part of me understood. I also knew, she was a good woman and looking at my daughter, she'd done an amazing job raising Cadence. *Wow I have another daughter.* I thought to myself, grinning. I wanted to scoop her up in my arms and let her know I'll never leave her.

"Ma?" Cadence called out, moving around in her hospital bed.

"Your mother stepped out for a few. Are you in pain? You want me to call the nurse?"

"No." Cadence stared at me. "You're my father aren't you?"

I nodded my head. "Yep."

"Where you been?" Cadence didn't waste any time getting down to it.

"Your mother and I lost communication. I can't apologize enough for that. But we found each other again and I'm so happy to find out about you."

"You didn't walk out on me?"

"No, sweetie. I never would've walked out on you. If you let me in your life, I promise to be there for you from now on. I would like a chance to be your father."

"Are you strict because Ma is a beast in Louboutin's."

I cracked up laughing. "Oh, you have my sense of humor."

"I heard." Cadence smiled.

"I'm not too bad, I don't think. You'll have to ask your sister and brothers. You have one sister and two brothers."

"For real? They live here too?"

"Nah, they live in Arizona but they'll be here this summer. I left before you were born and I recently moved back."

"Did you love my mother?"

"Yes and I still do." Cadence smiled hearing that. "I hope you like teddy bears, that's all they had in the gift shop."

"What girl doesn't like teddy bears. I'll put them on the shelf in my bedroom. Thank you, they're cute."

"Next time, I'll let you pick out what you want. But right now," I leaned forward so she could see the genuineness in my eyes. "I want you to tell me everything about yourself. Don't leave anything out."

Cadence and I spoke for what seemed like a lifetime. She was full of questions and so was I. This was a new chapter in my life and I felt truly blessed, to have an opportunity to get to know not only my daughter but my firstborn child.

After Cadence fell asleep, I left the hospital and headed straight to my father's house. When I pulled up, I saw Santi's truck. Just the nigga I wanted to see. I was on a mission and found his ass in the kitchen eating.

"Wassup Cross?" Santi mumbled with a mouth full of food.

I sat down for a few seconds not saying a word. I was fuming and I knew this shit was about to go all the way left, so I was mentally preparing myself.

"What's wrong wit' you?" Santi frowned his face at me.

"Santi, do you love your children?"

"What kind of question is that? Yeah I love my kids. What the hell is wrong wit' you?" he scoffed, biting down on his sandwich.

"I love my kids too."

"Okay! We love our kids. Duh!" Santi looked baffled.

"I trusted you and you stabbed me in the back. No, I take that back, you stabbed me in my heart."

"Nigga, what the fuck are you talkin' about? You drunk or something?"

"No! I'ma little fucked up in the head. I just met my sixteen year old daughter, who I knew nothing about. Thanks to you."

"Wait what?!" Santi almost choked on his sandwich.

"Years ago, I gave you a letter. I said take this letter to Tia's house. You remember that?"

"Yeah." A guilty look crept across Santi's face.

"But you didn't give it to her."

"I was on my way to take her the letter but I had a flat. Pop wasn't here because he was with you. So I asked Curtis Jr. if I could use his car, he said no because he had something to do. I damn near begged him but he wouldn't let me. I told him how important it was and he said he would drop it off for me. So I gave the letter to Curtis

Jr. He left, and when he came back, he said he handled it."

"But I told you not to let anyone know about the letter. I only trusted you with it."

"Man, I thought Curtis Jr. handled it. That's what he said. He had no reason to lie."

I shook my head at Santi. "Because I trusted you, Charly thought I dipped on her and didn't let me know she was pregnant. I had to meet my firstborn in a hospital bed."

"Cross, you gotta believe me man, I thought I was doing the right thing. I wouldn't do you wrong, not intentionally. But why would Curtis Jr. lie?"

"I don't know but he's gonna......."

"What Cross in here whining about now?" Curtis Jr. mocked, interrupting me coming into the kitchen.

I jumped up and rushed my brother knocking him to the stone flooring. "You punk ass muthafucka!" I roared.

"Nigga, what's wrong wit' you!" Curts Jr. hollered as he struggled to get free from my chokehold. Under normal circumstances, it probably wouldn't be too difficult since he was solid muscle but so was I and my rage was giving me superhero type strength. As I tried to tighten my grip, ready to break my brother's neck, the heel of my timberland boot slipped from something wet on the floor. Curtis took advantage of my loosened grasp by swinging on me. I regained my balance and we started exchanging blows. My last punch connected with Curtis right jaw causing him to tumble backwards and hit the floor.

Santi grabbed me from behind. "Chill out." He held me back while Curtis Jr. scrambled to his feet yelling obscenities.

"What in the hell is going on in here?" Pops stormed in the room and demanded to know.

Curtis Jr. attempted to charge towards me but our father stopped him. "Get your simple ass in the living room."

"What you screaming at me for?!" Curtis Jr. huffed, swinging at the air, cursing all the way into the living room.

"You two get in there!" Pops screamed.

Santi and I went into the living room but I didn't want to be anywhere near my brother. He was a trader as far as I was concerned.

"You even sucka punch like a soft ass nigga." Curtis Jr. taunted, as soon as I walked into the room.

"And you took them punches like a hoe nigga who like gettin' fucked up the ass," I shot back.

"Enough! Cross sit down and shut up. Santi you too!"

"I ain't do nothin." Santi mumbled as he slouched down next to me on the couch.

"Cross, what happened?"

"What you asking him for?" Curtis Jr. complained.

"Boy, shut up!" Pops looked back at me. "Now why you swinging on your brother in my house?"

I stared at Curtis Jr. while I attempted to control my anger. I had to stop looking at him. The smug expression on his face made me wanna pounce on him again. "Pop, it's a long story."

"I got time. You better get to talking, Cross. I'm losing my patience."

"Just tell him." Santi nudged me.

I went back almost seventeen years ago to the beginning. The letter. Running into Charly and clearing the air. Finding out she never got the letter. Then ultimately seeing Cadence for the first time and realizing I was her father.

Pop was silent for a while. "You didn't tell me there was a baby involved." He shot a look at

Curtis Jr.

"I didn't know about a baby. I just destroyed the letter like you told me to." Curtis Jr. admitted.

"Hold up! You knew about me and Charly?" I couldn't believe what I was hearing.

"Dad, that's fucked up." Santi moaned.

"I didn't know about a baby but I couldn't let you throw your life away on that girl." Pops tried to explain.

"That girl was your Goddaughter. That girl was family and that girl has a name and she didn't do a damn thing to you."

"Cross, I was protecting you."

"Protecting me from what?" I stood up waiting for my father to justify his actions.

"Had I known she was pregnant, I would've handled things differently."

"I can't decide who I'm more disgusted with. You or that simple nigga over there," I scoffed eyeing Curtis Jr. No longer being able to stomach my father or my brother, the only thing for me to do was walk away. I went upstairs to pack my bags. At first, I wasn't sure how I was going to break the news to my father, I'd gotten my own spot and was moving out but the bullshit him and Curtis Jr. pulled, gave me the perfect out.

"Cross, we need to talk about this." Pop stood in my doorway trying to continue our conversation but I had nothing left to say.

"I'm done." Were the only words I could muster up. I didn't want to hear anything else from my father. Looking at him made me want to forget everything I was taught growing up and beat him like he was the enemy. So I just kept packing up my things not acknowledging his presence.

"Croccifixio!" Pop screamed, stepping into my bedroom.

"Is Croccifixio here?" my mother walked slightly off balance into the room. "Cross...You came home."

I looked up and the sight of my mother walking towards me damn near brought me to tears.

"You came home." My mother repeated herself. She walked over to me and held my face and kissed me. "My special boy. You make me so proud. I love you Cross..."

"I love you too, mama." I hugged her so tight, I never wanted to let go. She laid her head on my chest. My mother was always a tiny woman but now she seemed even more fragile. Pop watched from over in the corner and he could see the disdain on my face.

"You just got here and you're leaving already?"

"No, I'm not leaving. Let's go back in your room so I can show you pictures of your grandbabies. You would like that right."

"Grandbabies? Cross...you have children?" my mother glanced around with a confused look on her face. "Where are they? Are they hiding?"

I put my arm around my mother and guided her back to her room. My heart sank with each step. She remembered me but not my kids.

"They don't live here but you'll see them when they come to visit."

"You promise?" my mother looked up at me with childlike eyes.

"I promise." I walked her back to her room and helped her get into bed. I stayed by her side and we talked for a long time. It became evident that my mother thought I had come home on college break. I showed her pictures of my children but I got pissed all over again when I had none of Cadence. Her eyes watered as she talked about how beautiful they were. As I witnessed her memory slipping away again, I put her favorite movie in. Imitation of life. We watched the entire film as she gave commentary on every scene. Then she drifted off to sleep. I tucked her in like she was a baby and kissed her on cheek. After watching her sleep peacefully for a while, I went back to my bedroom to finish packing my things and I got the hell out of there.

Chapter 9

Charly

I had to get away from everybody and clear my mind so I drove around for hours. I kept replaying my conversation with Cross and how he seemed to be filled with all this hatred towards me. I finally decided it was time I checked on Cadence.

"Hey baby girl. How you feeling?"

"Much better. I just woke up from a nap. I fell asleep after Cross left...I mean my dad," Cadence giggled. "I can't believe I have a father. I mean I always knew I had a father but to actually have him in my life."

I could see Cadence smiling through the phone. "I guess that means you and Cross got along pretty good."

"More like great. I know we're just getting to know each other but I already see so many similarities between us. I even have a sister and two brothers. I can't wait to meet them." Cadence was going on and on. I hadn't heard her sound this excited since daddy got her a baby Benz for her Sweet 16 birthday party.

"Cadence, I don't mean to interrupt but I need you to do me a favor," I said turning our upbeat chat serious.

"Sure, what is it?"

"I know you're ecstatic about meeting your father for the first time but please don't tell your grandfather about Cross. I wanna be the one to tell him. Will you do that for me?"

"Of course but don't take too long. I want everyone to meet my dad," Cadence announced proudly.

"I'm on it. Now you get some rest. I'll see you tomorrow. Love you."

After I got off the phone with Cadence, I drove around for another hour before heading to my father's house. I rehearsed what I was going to say the entire ride over. When I pulled up to his house, I took a deep breath and went inside.

"Hey, Daddy!" Daddy was sitting in his chair with a grimaced face.

"Where have you been? I've been calling you, Tia even came over here looking for you! Big Mike is out searching the streets as we speak!"

I sat down across from him in the chair. "I'm sorry. Daddy, I really am. I just needed to clear my head."

"You left my baby girl at the hospital alone. What the hell is wrong with you?"

"I didn't leave her by herself!" I snapped back, getting pissed off.

"Tia is not her mother, you are!" He barked.

"I left Cadence with her father! I shot back." This was not the way I had rehearsed my breaking news but fuck it. No man, not even my daddy was gonna keep talking to me like I was crazy.

"Her father? You left my baby girl alone in the hospital with a Payne!"

My eyes widened and I wasn't sure if I heard him correctly. "What did you say?"

"I didn't stutter. Have you lost your mind? You left Cadence alone with Cross Payne? Are you stupid?"

My eyes searched the air around me trying to figure out how daddy knew about Cross.

"Get that dumb expression off of yo' face. You think I didn't know Cross was my grand-daughter's father? I was there when Cross was born, with his jet black eyes like Lita. When you placed my baby girl in my arms and I saw her eyes, I knew who her father was."

"You've known this entire time?" I ran my hands over my face. "And you said nothing?" anger was stirring up inside of me.

"Why would I? I told you a Payne could not be trusted and you went behind my back and not only laid down with the enemy but had a child with him too."

My blood was pumping strong and my breathing was rapid. I thought my heart would jump out of my chest.

"Cross was not your enemy, Daddy! He's your Godson for goodness sake!"

"He's a Payne!" Daddy screamed and hit his fist on the arm of the chair.

"This is insane!" I was now standing up

flailing my arms around. "Cross and I shouldn't have to pay for some stupid vendetta you and Curtis have with each other. We were kids and we loved each other."

Daddy laughed and shook his head. "Love? Where was all of this love when you were pregnant? Or in the hospital giving birth?"

"He didn't even know I was pregnant. Cross didn't find out Cadence was his daughter until today."

"And you leave her alone with him. When did you become this stupid? I thought I raised you to be smarter than that. You are a disappointment, Charly." My father put his head down as if he wanted to disown me.

Daddy's words cut like a knife. *You better not cry. You better not cry.* I told myself.

"Charlie, you have gone too far." Miss Erma fussed coming in the room. "She has done nothing but try to please you, so stop with this nonsense. You've been giving this poor child a hard time since I met you." Miss Erma turned to me, "Baby, pay him no mind. You live your life. You're a smart girl and a good woman."

"Erma, stay in your place!" Daddy hollered at her. "This is between me and my daughter."

"My place?" Miss Erma put her hand on her wide hips. "Oh, I know my place, Charlie Brinx! I cook your food, I take care of you 24/7. I love this baby as if she was my own, and I keep your bed warm every night. So trust and believe I know my place!"

I looked at Miss Erma then at daddy then back at Miss Erma with my mouth wide open. "Wait what? Did she just say, you keep his bed warm every night? Miss Erma, you and Daddy?"

"Charlie, tell her or I will." Daddy stood speechless which was unheard of. In all the years I knew the man, he was never at a loss for words.

"Tell me what?" I looked to daddy for answers.

"I'm his wife!"

My knees started to buckle and I went down but Miss Erma caught me before I hit the floor. She helped me to the chair.

"Baby, I'm sorry. I wanted to tell you but your daddy wanted to keep it a secret." Miss Erma's voice was soothing as ever.

"But why? Why would I care? You've been nothing but good to me and Cadence. You're like my mom anyway. This doesn't make any sense."

"I told him that! See, Charlie! I told you!" Miss Erma walked over to daddy and smacked him in the back of his head. She sat down on the arm of his chair. "I love this stubborn olé' mule." Miss Erma laughed.

"Wow!" Was all I could say.

"Now apologize to Charly. She didn't deserve that tongue lashing you gave her. Go on now."

But being the stubborn man he was, my father remained mute. He wouldn't even look in my direction. "I guess only one of us is allowed to keep a secret. But wait, you already knew my truth, so I guess the lie is on you," I said before grabbing my purse and heading to the door.

"Baby, where you going? Don't leave! Charlie don't let that Chile walk out the door," Miss Erma pleaded.

I knew my father wouldn't stop me, he was too stuck on stupid. "It's okay Miss Erma," I said as I opened the front door and left.

Miss Erma came out after me. "Baby girl, I don't know what to say. He's an old fool but he's our old fool."

"It is what it is. I'm used to not living up to his expectations. I will never be the son he always wanted. So it's whatever." I shrugged.

Miss Erma placed her loving hands on my face. "Don't ever let me hear you say that again. You have exceeded your father's expectations. He's too stubborn to tell you but he's told me time and time again. So stop chasing a ghost, you are and have always been more than enough."

"Thank you Miss Erma." We embraced and I got in the car and drove off. I picked up my iPhone and was tempted to call Cross but changed my mind. Instead, I decided to go back to the hospital and spend the night there with Cadence.

As I was coming out of my sleep, I heard voices. I shifted in the bed slowly opening my eyes. I woke up to Cadence and Cross engaged in a conversation. I just listened instead of letting them know I was awake or even in the room.

"She seems like a nice lady. Imitation Of Life is one of my favorite movies too." Cadence told Cross.

Cross turned his lips up. "What you know about that movie?" Cross had a silly grin on his face staring at our daughter.

"I'm a movie buff. That's a classic...thank you

very much." They both laughed simultaneously. Cadence and Cross had bonded and there was no help necessary on my end.

Damn my leg hurt I thought to myself while trying to listen intently to Cross and Cadence's conversation. As I turned my body to get more comfortable in the cramped bed, my purse dropped on the floor.

"'Ma! I had no idea you were in that other bed. How long have you been here?" Cadence asked, stunned to see me. From the glare on Cross's face, I could tell he was surprised and not pleased.

"I got here last night but you were knocked out. You had the room to yourself, so I decided to sleep in this bed. I wanted to be here when you woke up."

"I'm glad you're here. Now I have both my parents to keep me company," Cadence beamed.

"Good Morning! I need to check the patient," the doctor said, walking in with the nurse. I was relieved there entrance interrupted our family moment. "How are you feeling?" the doctor asked Cadence.

"I feel good. Can I go home?"

"After I examine you we'll talk about it.

How's that?"

"Cool," Cadence nodded.

"After the examination I want to run a few more routine test on your daughter. Nothing for you to worry about but it will take a while in case you want to go to the cafeteria and have some breakfast, " the doctor suggested.

"Ma, can you go get me some McDonald's."

"Sure. I want to make a Starbucks run anyway," I said getting my purse off the floor. "Call me if you need anything else," I told Cadence before stepping out the room.

Cross stood in the hallway seemingly in deep thought. It was obvious he was still angry with me but I was willing to humble myself because I wanted to make things right.

"You wanna go get something to eat and talk?" Cross seemed reluctant. "This is difficult for me but I'm trying. Please meet me half way."

Cross didn't say a word but his actions showed he was willing to try, when he walked out the hospital with me. I told him to follow me home. That way I could shower, change and we would have some privacy because I was positive our talk was going to get heated.

"Make yourself at home," I told him as we entered my house.

"This is nice, Charly. What you hired an interior decorator?"

"No," I chuckled. "I did it myself."

"Really? This looks like one of those homes in a magazine or a HGTV show."

"Thank you. I always wanted to do interior design. It's my passion."

"You definitely have the skills."

"Thanks. I'ma take a quick shower and then I'll make us something to eat, so we can talk. Feel free to make yourself at home."

"No problem, take your time."

I imagined myself soaking in a relaxing bubble bath to bring down my stress level but I settled on a shower, since I was starving and I knew Cross was too. As the hot water drenched my body, I tried to figure out exactly what I needed to say, so I could make things right with Cross. The conversation with my dad went all the way left and I wanted to avoid that happening all over again.

"That was much quicker than I expected," Cross commented after I came back downstairs, went into the kitchen and started cooking.

"Don't know about you but I get pretty grumpy when I'm hungry," I said, as I put potatoes and onions in one pan, bacon on the griddle while scrambling eggs in a bowl.

"Or maybe you simply prefer coming up with excuses to be mad," Cross replied nonchalantly, as he was sitting down checking his phone.

I ignored his jab and continued cooking. I made us coffee, fixed our plates and we ate pretty much in silence. I couldn't speak for Cross but I know my thoughts were scattered. He looked up and caught me watching him.

"I think we should talk," I finally said, staring at him over my coffee cup.

"I agree. I'ma let you start." Cross pushed his plate away and folded his arms.

"I see you're still on the defense but I can't blame you," I conceded. "I was an emotional wreck yesterday seeing my baby in a hospital bed. My nerves were raw, so I admit, I should've handled things differently and I'm sorry. But for what it's worth, I was going to tell you about Cadence."

"It's easy for you to say that now, since the truth is out. When did you plan on telling me about my daughter, in the next few weeks or another sixteen years? Charly, I don't even think you realize how fucked up it is what you did. You denied my child her father and me the opportunity to be a positive influence in her life."

"You're right." I put my head down because I became consumed with guilt. Cross was robbed and more importantly so was Cadence. For all these years, I saw myself as a victim but it was never me. Cross and our daughter were the ones deprived of a relationship for all these years.

"Acknowledging I'm right, doesn't change anything, Charly."

"It does for me. It wasn't until this very moment did I grasp the severity of the decision I made, by keeping the truth from you. Maybe initially, I could blame it on youth. Being a teenage mother wasn't easy. Mixed with shame because my father always warned me to stay away from the Paynes. Not only did I lose my virginity to a Payne but I gave my heart to you too. Then, I wake up and you're gone. I felt devastated and betrayed," I divulged as a tear escaped my eye. The pain of that day was still so fresh in my mind. As I tried to wipe my face, Cross reached over and took my hand.

"I get it," Cross said, caressing the side of my cheek. "I don't wanna hang on to my anger any longer. I can't get back those sixteen years with my daughter but I can make sure I don't waste any more time."

"Does that mean you forgive me?" I asked.

"Yes, I forgive you and I also want to thank you."

"Thank me for what?"

"For raising such a sweet and beautiful kid. Cadence seems to be an amazing young lady. You've done a great job and I want to move forward. Plus, life is way too short and unpredictable to stay mad." Cross's eyes seemed to be heavy in thought, as if the last part had an even deeper meaning.

"I appreciate what you said regarding Cadence but are you ok? I mean I know yesterday was an emotional rollercoaster ride but your energy is off."

"You noticed huh?" Cross let out a long sigh before opening up and sharing with me everything that happened at his father's house. When he spoke about his mother he started to tear up.

I walked over and held him. I wanted Cross to know it was okay to let it out. He cried and I couldn't help but cry with him because I had a lot of love for Miss Lita. She was a quiet woman but as sweet as they came. My heart hurt for Cross.

"I'm sorry." Cross straightened up and wiped his face. "I can't believe I cried in front of you."

"Don't apologize. I'll never understand why men think crying is a sign of weakness. Maybe out there in those streets but not with me. It's safe here."

Cross looked up at me and saw I had been crying too. He wiped my tears away. "We'll get through this."

"Hopefully together because I need you," I told Cross and then gave him a blow by blow of what happened with my own father too.

"Charly, I'm sorry to hear that," he shook his head. "I know how close you and your dad are. "What the hell is wrong with our fathers?" Cross became aggravated.

"They're both too old and stubborn to change."

"Shit, that's on them. We can't make them act right and they can no longer influence our decisions."

"True but it does complicate business."

"Why should it? We both know how to separate business from our personal lives," Cross
reasoned.

"My dad might not want me to continue
running things."

"I doubt it. Charlie talks a lot of shit but he
only trust you."

"To be honest, I don't care anymore. I'm
ready to make an exit out the game," I stood
up and said. "I have no intentions of letting Cadence join the family business. I've done my
best to shield her from this life but the streets
be talking. She's no longer a little girl, more like
an inquisitive teenager."

"I get what you saying but making a clean
exit out the game isn't as easy as you think.
For now, just take it one day at a time. But we
probably need to get back to the hospital and
bring Cadence her food."

"Yeah, we better go but before we do, are
we good?"

"Charly, I told you all is forgiven. I wanna
put that behind us and move forward and focus
on being a father to Cadence."

"I'm talking about us, Cross. Are we good?" I stressed the we, pointing my finger at the both of us.

Instead of answering my question with words, Cross showed me with his actions. He stepped towards me, lifted up my face so I could stare into his hypnotic eyes. He was the only man who could make me feel like a love struck teenager, without uttering a word. He leaned down and pressed his soft lips against mine. Cross kiss started slow and sweet but ended with intense passion. I had my man back but this time I would do things right because I had no intention of ever letting him go.

Chapter 10

Cross

Pops was in his office when I arrived. I headed straight to my mother's room. "How's the most beautiful woman in the world?" I leaned in and kissed her on the cheek. My mother looked up at me and I could tell by the empty glare in her eyes, she didn't have a clue who I was.

"Do I know you?"

"It's me, Ma...Cross." I sat down with her and tried to make her understand who I was.

"You're not my son. I would remember my own son."

Those words cut deep but I understood it was her illness talking. So after swallowing the pain I asked my mother if I could sit with her while she watched television. I think I spent more time watching her then the TV.

When my father came in to give mother her medicine, we didn't speak. Instead, we sat in silence keeping vigil over her until the medicine kicked in and she fell asleep.

"Meet me in my office." Pop summoned, giving me little choice in the matter.

I took a deep breath and gathered my thoughts before going downstairs to his office.

"Have a seat, Cross." Pop gestured for me to sit down. I obliged and did as he said. "How's your daughter doing?"

"Cadence is good she's back home, a little sore but she'll be okay."

"She's my granddaughter and I know you don't believe me but I do love my children and my grandchildren." There was a softness in my father's voice that I wasn't used to hearing. "Cross, I did what I thought was best for you. You had a full ride and all I could see was you throwing your life away for a girl. Was I wrong? Yes. I should've come to you but I did not know anything about a baby. I wouldn't rob you of your own child.

And when I found out Charlie was a grandfather the baby was already here and I didn't put two and two together. No matter what you think of me, you should know, if I'd known I had a grandchild out there, I wouldn't stay away. Which is probably why Charlie made sure I didn't know about it."

"Charly never told him who the father was," I explained, choosing to leave out that he figured it out.

"I would like to meet her, get to know my granddaughter. Is that something you can arrange? Will Charly be ok with that? I know her father won't go for it."

"Cadence wants to meet you too and Charly is cool with it, as long as our daughter isn't put in a tug of war. We both want the best for her and Charly is her own woman, so it doesn't really matter if Charlie likes it or not."

"I know Charly can hold her own. She's been making major moves since taking over for her father. She's always been headstrong like her old man too," Pops chuckled.

"See, you just thought back to how things were when we were a family didn't you? Charly is her father's daughter but she is still the same girl you considered your little girl. Our love for each other is bigger than this stupid beef between you and Charlie. Can't you see that?"

"Cross, I wish things were different I really do but it's too much water under the bridge and the water is dirty. But you have my word, I won't take my animosity out on Cadence. She's innocent in all this."

"I guess that's a start."

"Have you talked to the other kids about Cadence yet?"

"No, I'm doing it today."

"Are you and Charly together now?"

"Yes we are." I watched his face closely to see if his expression changed.

"I figured. I'm not trying to argue with you but I can't have our family business shared with Charly."

"I understand. We've already discussed keeping business and our personal relationship separate. We're in agreeance on that," I made clear.

"I hope you understand I want you to be happy. I really do, that's why I pushed so hard for you to get an education. I knew I would need to depend on you to take over one day. Curtis Jr. acts too much like me and Santiago, well he can't even commit to one woman let alone run a business. But you, you are the one and if Andrew had lived, you two would have worked side by side. I know that's a heavy weight to carry and I also know you didn't choose this. But who better then you, to begin transitioning everything to legitimate enterprises."

"I can make it happen. I'm glad that's the direction you want to go in."

"I'm thinking within a year or so, we can have everything legal," Pop said, rubbing his temples.

"You a'ight?"

"I can't get rid of this headache."

"You're barely sleeping. You doing too much. You need help taking care of mom. Get a qualified nurse to come in."

"I'll think about it. I could use some help though."

"Then do it. We'll get round the clock care here and you'll be able to sleep through the night, go out without having to find somebody to watch over mother. I'll even interview potential caregivers. It's worth a try. If you don't like it, you can always pull the plug."

"Do you see why I need you around?"

"I do. We might have our differences but I won't ever turn my back on our family. Family is all we got. You taught me that," I stated as Pop and I embraced. "I'll bring Cadence to see you soon. That's a promise."

I left my father's house and headed straight to Charly. I wanted to spend time with both of them as a family. When I was about to get out the car, my phone started to ring. "Yeah," I answered, without looking to see who was calling.

"What's good?" Curtis Jr.'s voice echoed on speaker phone.

"Chillin' what's up?" my response was guarded. I was always guarded with my brother because he was too unpredictable.

"Santi said he met your daughter."

"Yeah, he stopped by the hospital before she was discharged."

"Somebody could've included me on the family reunion."

"I didn't know he was coming. He just showed up."

"Oh, so are you gonna let me meet her?"

"When she can get around, I'll bring her out to the house so everybody can meet her."

"A'ight cool. You staying in the city now?"

"Yep, I gotta spot."

"I'm gonna have to come by and check you out."

"No doubt, just hit me up. I'm still getting it together but it's straight."

"After my meeting with my lawyer tomorrow I'll swing by. Just text me the address."

"Will do."

"And let me know when you gonna bring your daughter out. I wanna wrangle up my kids so they can be there. You know I gotta hunt those lil' niggas down until they want some money."

Curtis Jr. had four kids, two boy's, two girls. One positive thing I can say about him, is that he was a good father. He started out early becoming a dad at 15 but he stepped up to the plate and he's still with Pam. I never understood why they never got married though.

"I feel you. I'll def let you know.

"A'ight bruh I'll get at you tomorrow."

"Cool!" I ended the call but this eerie feeling came over me. I brushed it off and headed into the house so I could be with Cadence and Charly. My family needed me and I needed them too.

Chapter 11

Charly

I felt like I was dreaming. So many nights when I was pregnant with Cadence, I imagined Cross coming back for us. And now my dream had become a reality. Laying in his arms after making love, had my heart full.

I glanced over at Cross and he was sound asleep. Me on the other hand was wide awake. My love life feeling so perfect, had me extra giddy and wide awake. Since I couldn't sleep, I reached for my phone and sent Tia a text.

You up

Tia didn't text back, instead she called.

"Hey girl!" I said,trying to keep my voice down so I wouldn't wake Cross.

"What you doing up?"

"Girl, I couldn't sleep, so I decided to harass yo' ass," I laughed. Many nights Tia and I would spend hours on the phone in the middle of the night. It was feeling like old times again.

"Well, I'm up so harass me all you like," she giggled. "Where's Cross?"

"He's right here sleeping." I looked over my shoulder at him.

"I got something to tell you." Tia's voice sounded nervous. "Promise not to get mad and flip out on me."

"Oh Lawd! Girl, what did you do?" I sat straight up in my bed.

"Promise!"

"Bitch, you know I promise. Now tell me! You got me anxious." I shouted a little too loud. I glanced back at Cross to see if I had awakened him.

"I'm in my living room talking to you, so I don't wake him."

"Oh, you got company...do tell...do tell," I teased.

Tia seemed to be hesitating. "It's Santi."

I laid back down in the bed and put the covers slightly over my mouth before I went in on Tia. "What! You fuckin' Santiago?" I hissed.

"Sssh, bitch damn! I said don't flip out. Please don't be mad," she pleaded.

"Girl, I'm not mad, not even surprised to be honest. When he came to visit Cadence at the hospital, I saw how chummy the two of you were being. I said to myself, that nigga 'bout to talk Tia out her panties," I chuckled. "Plus Santi your type, tatted up, gangsta and shit."

"Don't remind me. I was supposed to leave those type of dudes alone."

"You like what you like. Why you think you get bored so easily with these straight laced Fortune 500 dudes. You crave excitement."

"You know me so well. I just knew you were gonna flip because you're wary of the Paynes."

"I still am. I do get a good vibe off of Santi though. He is Cross's brother and if Cross trusts him, that's good enough for me."

"Oh wow! Is my best friend sprung?! You're following Cross's lead?"

"I know right but I believe in Cross."

"Awww you sound so cute, all in love and shit."

"Shut up! I'm still that bitch, don't get it twisted but I'll admit it feels good to be in love and have a man I can rely on. Shit even a bad bitch deserves a break and needs backup."

"I know that's right. I'm happy for you Charly and Cadence. And I can see how much he loves you too. Girl, that man look at you like Victor look at Nikki on the Young and the Restless," Tia laughed.

"You stupid!" Cross started to rub my inner thigh. "Well go on back to your company. We'll talk later."

"Ok girl, I'll be over in the morning."

"A'ight."

"Love you."

"Love you too." I ended the call and put my phone down. Cross's hand was still on my thigh and he used it to pull me closer. His body was so warm. I wanted to stay wrapped up next to him forever. "I didn't mean to wake you."

"It's cool. I'm glad you did," he said as we shared a kiss, then we had pillow talk about Tia and Santi.

"I hope this Tia and Santi hookup doesn't go bad. I mean she's like my sister, he's your brother. Family functions could get real awkward."

"We already got that covered with our fathers so they'll blend right in," Cross chuckled.

"True that!"

"I will say, Santi's track record with women is sketchy at best. Hopefully Tia won't become another casualty."

"Don't worry, your brother has met his match with Tia," I winked.

"Say no more. Enough about them, it's all about us right now." Cross kissed me on the lips before taking his tongue action between my legs. I was already so wet at just the thought of him being inside of me. I began to moan. I loved when Cross had me under his spell. It was the only time my mind and body was in complete ecstasy.

"It took you forever." I fussed when I opened the door for Tia.

"I know I ain't shit but the dick had me wide open." Tia confessed as she sashayed into the house. She made herself comfortable next to me on the couch. Poured herself a glass of mimosa from the pitcher I had on the table. "Where's Cross and Candy?"

"Cadence was feeling much better today and decided to go run some errands with her dad."

"Nice!" Tia smiled, taking a sip of her drink.

"Mmmhmmm. So anyway," I crossed my legs Indian style, "You and Santi." I shook my head at her.

"I know, I know but it just happened."

"How did it just happen? You slipped and fell on his dick?"

"Yep over and over and over again." Tia hit my leg as she laughed.

"Just be careful, Santi's a heartbreaker."

"I know, he was very open about how he gets down. But he's fun and baby when I tell you he can put it down!" Tia gyrated in her seat.

"As long as you know what you're getting into." Tia was a man eater. I've seen her chew up some of the best guys and spit them out but Santi was a different kind of animal. This could either go really good or really bad.

"I do. I'm moving with caution. But what you looking at on your laptop...are those houses?"

Tia was letting me know she was ready to stop talking about Santiago and move on to the next subject.

"Yes! Cross and I want to move in together but we want to start fresh, so I'm looking at potential houses. "I'm about to head out shortly. Are you coming with?"

"Do you even have to ask." Tia frowned up her face. "You know I am. I'm surprised Cross not coming."

"He said he trust my taste. He only wants to see my final three choices and then he'll give his input on which house he likes best."

"My kinda guy," Tia smirked pouring her third mimosa.

"Girl, I know you a drunk but try to save me a glass," I joked, before going upstairs to get my purse, so we could leave.

I don't know if the mimosa had us tipsy or we were so caught up in our laughing and giggling we didn't notice a dark colored SUV drive pass my house twice. It wasn't until it came circling back the third time and the passenger window slowly rolled down, did I know things were about to go bad.

"Tia get down!" I yelled, yanking her arm.

We both lunged our bodies to the ground and began crawling towards my car.

"Oh fuck! Them muthafuckas shooting at us!" Tia yelped as bullets kept spraying in our direction.

"Just keep crawling towards the car. I got one of my guns in the glove department," I told Tia. I was pissed I didn't have nothing in my purse. I changed them so much, I would just always keep a weapon in my crib and both my cars. I figured when I was on the move, I could retrieve it from my car and put it in whatever purse I was carrying at the time. Now I was out here being ambushed with no protection.

When the SUV went in reverse and then turned in the driveway my heart dropped. It was like they wanted to guarantee they finished us off. I was tempted to stand up and run towards my car but I knew it meant an automatic death sentence.

"Charly, we 'bout to die," Tia cried out. "I love you so much. Don't you ever forget that," she continued to weep.

"I love you too," I called out but I wasn't ready to die. I was trying to figure out how I could get us out this shit but we needed a miracle. That miracle showed up in the form of Cross. His black on black Range Rover pulled up spraying bullets. When one of the slugs made contact with the driver of the SUV, I heard a loud screeching sound and the truck sped off.

Tia and I both laid on our backs staring up at the sky. The bright sun beamed down on us as we thanked God for sparing our lives.

Chapter 12

Cross

"I gave you the tag number. I want you to find out who the fuck was in that truck!" I roared. "Call me back wit' that information cause by this time tomorrow, I want all them muthafuckas dead!" I threw my phone down on the couch and went upstairs to check on Charly.

"Did you find out anything?" Charly asked, when I walked in the bedroom..

"No, I got nothing so far. But luckily I memorized the license plate number. Trust me, I'ma find out who's behind this."

"Thank God, you had dropped Cadence off over at Diamond's house. If she had been in the car with you..." Charly's voice trailed off and she sat down on the bed.

"Baby, it's okay. Cadence wasn't with me and she's safe. I got two of my men parked outside Diamond's house. Nobody is gonna touch our daughter."

"Being in this game, I've had some close calls but never nothing like this," Charly shook her head. "I really thought me and Tia were gonna die," she looked up at me and said.

"But you not dead." I wrapped my arms around Charly. I wanted her to feel safe.

"Only because of you. Cross, if you hadn't showed up..."

"But I did," I said, cutting Charly off. "You finish packing so we can get outta here. You and Cadence will stay at my penthouse until we find our new house. Don't worry I got you," I reassured Charly and kissed her on the forehead.

"You moving on up, ain't you lil bruh," Curtis Jr. cracked, when I came in the lobby to bring him up. He flashed his famous smile and we embraced.

"I'm doing a lil' something."

"I see!"

We got on the elevator and stepped off on my floor. Curtis Jr. put his fist up to his mouth and screamed. "Yo!!! This is fire!" As he looked around.

"Let me show you around."

"I'm feeling this Cross, real talk."

"Thanks," I said taking our seats. "Just got a delivery of food. You want some?" I offered.

"What you got for me?"

"I know you like oxtails." I pushed the container over to him.

"Ah yeah! And stuffed cabbage too. Das wassup!"

"I'll eat this jerk chicken." We dug into our food.

"You home alone?" Curtis questioned. "I know you mentioned Charly and Cadence were staying wit' you now after that shooting went down. Have you found out who was behind that shit yet?"

"Nah. They had stolen tags on the truck. But I got my men on it. Charly took Cadence over to her father's house. Cadence really wanted to spend some time wit' her grandfather."

"Oh." Curtis Jr. nodded.

"So, what the lawyer say?" I asked, switching the subject.

Curtis Jr. looked up from his food. "Man, he wants me to take a plea deal."

"What kind of time you looking at?"

"Shit five out dis bitch."

"Damn Jr.! What are your chances at trial?"

"10 to 12."

"That's fucked up." I shook my head.

"It's my damn fault. Pop stay on me about my temper."

I continued to shake my head. I didn't know what to say about that. Jr. never listens anyway. "So what you gonna do?"

"I ain't decided yet. I might take it to trial. You never know, one of the jurors could develop a soft spot for me. I'll take a hung jury. I doubt the prosecutor would wanna roll the dice twice," Curtis Jr. remarked sarcastically.

"Pop talkin' 'bout he was gonna speak to Francesco."

"What the fuck he gotta do wit' this shit?"

"Come on now, he the head of the organization."

"Nah, he the head of our lives. Fuck that muthafucka! He don't give a fuck about us. Shit! We his blood and he don't even claim our asses. We just niggas on the grind for him!"

I couldn't believe the venom Curtis Jr. was spitting towards Francesco.

"Don't look at me like that. You know I'm fuckin' right! Pops all scared of his ass! I ain't scared of his ass. I'll make a mufucka bleed one way or another."

I tilted my head and looked at my brother. There was something ominous in his tone.

"So you and shorty huh? Living together, playing house and shit."

"Yeah....." I don't know why but I suddenly became unnerved.

Jr. nodded his head as if he was thinking about something. "Yo! I need you to look after my seeds for me when I'm gone. You know keep em out of trouble. That boy of mine acts a lot like me and I don't want him to end up in the next cell, ya feel me?"

"No doubt, I got your back. But you ain't

locked up yet. Things might turn around."

"Maybe...maybe not. I got money put away for them. I just need you to make sure they are straight with the emotional shit and all that."

"You my brother. Those my nieces and nephews. I got you."

"I'm glad you back. Pops is losing his edge and Francesco has noticed, you better believe that! But since the 'smart guy' is back that gives us some leverage."

"There you go with that 'smart guy' shit."

"My dude, I'm proud of you. Shit you went off to school and got all these damn degrees and shit. You think me and Santiago could have done that? Andrew maybe but not us."

The mention of our deceased brother Andrew brought a sadness between us. We rarely talked about him because it upset our mother too much.

"So, what ex-wifey think about your new family? Damn, this stuffed cabbage is good as fuck." Jr. licked the juice off his fingers.

"She's in her feelings but shit, it's not like I knew and was hiding it. She'll be a'ight. Hell, I'm shocked too but unlike her, I'm happy about it."

"What about the kids?"

"My boys didn't react much, Kayla seemed to be cool with the idea of having a sister. She's a teenager you can never tell with them."

"I feel ya! If I take the plea, I gotta turn myself in within four weeks or some shit. I'm gonna try to get them to push it back as much as possible. Carlos got a baby coming and I want to be there to see my first grandchild."

"Shit, I didn't know that?"

"Yeah I'm gonna be a Pop-Pop." Jr. laughed. "I don't trust that little trick he got pregnant though, so I'm really gonna need you to make sure they're straight."

"Wow! I can't believe you gonna be somebody's grandfather."

"Fuck that, I'm Pop-Pop."

"Yeah ok Pop-Pop." I chuckled.

"We definitely need to have a family get together before then. Just us tho cuz, you know Pop gonna try to include those mufuckas that don't give a shit about us."

"You still on that?"

"You were away doing the college thing smart guy. I was the one at Pops side, so I had a front row seat to the blatant disrespect. Shit, have we EVER been invited to a family function? EVER?"

Jr. had a point. I never really thought of it like that before. "I guess you have a valid point."

"Yeah I do, so fuck them! The only time we invited over there is for a damn meeting. And even then they don't acknowledge us as family. That's disrespectful as hell. I can't tell you the last time any of them came to see our Mother so fuck Francesco and his bitch ass sons. Especially Luca."

"Man, Luca's a'ight."

"Was he a'ight when he was fuckin' the shit out of Charly?"

My face stiffened. "What you say?"

"You didn't know about Luca and Charly?"

"Nah, I don't know shit about that."

"You wouldn't, Luca not gonna let that shit get out."

I clinched my jaw to fight back the anger rising up in me. I couldn't believe Charly kept that shit from me.

"How you know about it then?"

"I make it my business to know what those mufuckas are doing. They were going kinda heavy some years back, meeting up at hotels and shit but like I said that was a while ago. I'm sure Charly was gonna come clean wit' you one day."

I wanted to knock the smug look off of Jr.'s face. He was enjoying telling me this news way too much. "I don't care about that shit." I lied and tried to convince myself at the same time.

"I know you don't, lil bruh," he pushed my shoulder on some playful shit. "I'm just telling you to watch ya back, cuz I don't know what Charly got between her legs but she had his ass wide open."

"Don't get fucked up!" I warned my brother.

Jr. threw his hands up. "I'm just saying. No disrespect. It's all love."

"Whatever! Watch yo' fuckin' mouth! Charly is my woman and the mother of my child. She ain't some broad I'm just fuckin'...remember that."

"Point made but Cross, watch Luca. He's more like Francesco than you know."

My brother was a hothead but he ain't never had a problem speaking his truth, good or bad. If he was warning me about Luca, then he was now on my radar.

Chapter 13

Charly

"I'm not pleased with how you are handling things in your personal life and I don't approve of your relationship with Cross but Erma made me see, I can't run your personal life. But this business is MINE and the second I see your personal life interfere with MY business, you're gone."

It wasn't what daddy said it was how he said it. I was beyond hurt from the contempt in his voice, I was furious.

"I guess you've forgotten that Cross saved my life and Tia's."

"I haven't forgotten shit. I placed a call to Cross and thanked him. It don't change nothing. He still the enemy as far as I'm concerned."

"The enemy that saved your daughter's life."

"You laying up in the bed wit' him. You the mother of one of his children. He did what any half ass nigga supposed to do," my dad scoffed.

"I can't win with you," I exhaled, throwing my hands up.

"Win?" he frowned. "I didn't realize we was playing some type of game. If we are let me know, cause I don't' lose at shit."

"I didn't mean it like that." My face scowled up. "If you no longer trust me, I don't have a problem stepping down."

"Did I say I didn't trust you? I made it clear where I stand. Keep the Payne's out of my business and we good."

I wanted to say much more but I decided against it. As pissed as I was with my daddy, I would never disrespect him.

There was a knock at the door and Cadence came in walking slow. A big smile came across daddy's face.

"Baby girl!"

"Hey granddaddy, I'm back!" Cadence made her way over to daddy and hugged him gently.

"I thought you had laid down to take a nap?"

"I did but I was feeling some discomfort, so I got up to take a pain pill."

"Cadence, we need to go home, so you can get some rest. You've been doing too much," I said.

"I agree with your mother. You did just have surgery. You need to take it easy."

"I know but I've missed you and I worry about you." Cadence started to cry.

"No tears, baby girl. I've missed you too. Look at me." Daddy lifted Cadence's face with his finger. His voice was calm but that's how he always was with Cadence.

"You focus on getting better, so you can come over and spend lots of time with your grandfather. I'm getting up in age but I ain't going nowhere."

"You promise?"

"Yes, I promise. Now I want you to go home and get in the bed and relax. I don't know why your mother allowed you to come over." Daddy shot me a disapproving look.

"I let her come because she loves you and she wanted to see you." I snapped. "Cadence, where's Tia?"

"I saw her in the kitchen with Miss Erma."

"Go get your stuff together and let Tia know we about to get ready to go. I want to talk to your grandfather about some business," I lied.

"Okay. I'm gonna call you later, Granddaddy." Cadence kissed him bye.

"Ok, be good." Daddy smiled.

"I will." Cadence turned around and looked at me. "I'll be waiting for you in the living room."

"Okay, I'll be out shortly." I waited for Cadence to close daddy's office door.

"Cadence shouldn't be out this much. She needs to get her strength back up."

"I agree. But you didn't leave me much of a choice. I wanted her to stay home and rest. But she insisted on seeing her grandfather. I couldn't bring myself to tell her, that you refused to come visit because we're now living at her father's house."

My father refused to acknowledge what I said. Instead he politely dismissed me. "You go take Cadence home. Call me if you need me. You know I love you."

"I know and I love you too."

Daddy and I looked at each other and smiled. We both knew that was as good as it was going to get between us for now. My father was a hard man and I had accepted that a long time ago.

I left my father's house frustrated. I knew him well enough to know it was going to take some time for him to get over Cross being in my life. That weighed heavy on my heart. I loved my dad more than anything but I was in love with Cross. All I wanted to do at this moment, was escape into the arms of my man and forget this mess. Cross made me so happy. I glimpsed in the rearview mirror as I changed lanes and I could actually feel myself smiling. But that's what he did for me, put a smile on my face.

The moment we got home, Cadence went upstairs. "Tia, I'll be right back. I want to check on Cadence before she goes to bed. She was already changing into her pajamas by the time I got to her bedroom. "Your medicine must be kicking in. You'll be knocked out sleep the second your face hits the pillow."

"Yeah, I am tired."

"You didn't say much on the ride home, are you okay? I know it must be difficult us having to leave our home abruptly and now we're living here with Cross. It's always been us girls against the world. Now you have a father in your life. Are you having a hard time adjusting to that? You know you can be honest with me, Cadence. Your feelings always come first."

"It's like I'm happy and you're happy but granddaddy isn't happy for us. He's not saying it but I can feel it. Plus, he's never hid his resentment towards the Payne family. I want to ask him so bad, don't you love me more then you hate the Payne's? And technically I'm a Payne, so does he still love me?"

"Don't you ever question your grandfather's love. You are his favorite person in the world. He'll be alright and so will anybody else who has a problem with us being a family. Your happiness is our priority. We're all devoted to you and that includes your grandfather." I could see Cadence's eyes becoming glassy. "Those pills are kicking in huh?"

"Yeah...." Cadence giggled batting her eyes.

I leaned over and kissed her on the forehead. "Get some rest, baby. And we're just gonna go with the flow." I put my pinky out and she wrapped hers around mine. Before I got out the door, I turned back to look at Cadence and she already started to drift off to sleep.

When I came back downstairs, Tia was sitting in the living room with an open bottle of wine.

"Girl, you are such a lush but this is exactly what I need right now." I sat down next to Tia. I let out a long sigh as I poured myself a glass of wine.

"So did you make up with your daddy?"

"Tia, that man," I shook my head. "You know how much I adore him but I am so angry right now. Do you know my child just asked me if daddy loved her more then he hates the Payne's."

"Ah damn! I hate that."

"Who you telling? Then she said since she's technically a Payne does he not love her anymore. That shit broke my heart."

"Maybe you should tell him how you feel."

I turned my lips up at Tia. "We are talking about OG Charlie Brinx. That man, ugh!" My phone vibrating interrupted our conversation. "Hold on a sec...yeah?"

"We need some help over here with this cleanup crew?" Slick told me.

"A'ight." I ended the call with Slick and called Big Mike and told him to come over now. Clean-up crew was our code for when the trap house gets hit and they know who did it. I then placed a call downstairs to the doorman to inform him I was expecting Big Mike and let him right up.

"Damn, Charly, your entire vibe changed."

"It's just business, Tia. "You know how it goes." I cut my eyes at her.

"I know, I know. But anyway, I was thinking you and Cross could use some alone time. I can stay here with Candy while you two go out, let your hair down and have some fun."

"I don't know. Cadence was in a lot of pain today. But I'll take a raincheck."

"Nah sis, you are stressed and I can see it all over your face. You should be on cloud nine right now being in love with the man whose been holding your heart captive all these years but you got your mind on business and your crazy ass daddy. I just don't want you to miss out on enjoying love."

"You're right! Cadence is in good hands with you. I thought he would've been home when we got here. Let me call Cross and see if he wants to."

"If Cross wants to what?" Cross asked walking through the door.

"Hey, babe. There you are," I smiled. I could tell by the look on his face, something was bothering him.

"Hey, Cross." Tia greeted him.

"Wassup. If Cross wants to what?" He repeated himself.

"Tia thinks we need to go out and have a good time. What you think?"

"Don't worry, I'll keep an eye on Candy." Tia told him.

"Let me think about it. Is Cadence sleep?" Cross headed upstairs.

"Yeah she's knocked out."

"What's wrong with him?"

I shrugged. "I'm about to find out though."

"Well, I'ma head on out. Call me if you decide to take me up on my offer."

I walked Tia to the door. "A'ight, I'll call you."

"Ok, love you."

"Back atcha!"

As Tia was getting on the elevator, Big Mike was getting off. I waited for him at the door. I was about to invite him in but Big Mike looked up and my eyes followed to see what he was staring at. I saw Cross standing on top of the wraparound staircase. The glare on Big Mike's face spoke volumes. Seeing Cross put him on edge.

"Babe, I'll be right back. I need to discuss some business with Big Mike," I explained. Cross didn't say a word, he turned and walked away. I closed the door behind me and got to it because I wanted to find out what was going on with my man.

"What you need, Boss Lady?"

"For one, I don't know what the hell is wrong with Slick calling me on my damn phone. He knows better. Two, he said he needs some help over with the cleanup crew in his spot."

"He got hit?"

"Yep! He's fuckin' up."

"So how you want to handle it?"

"Make every last one of those muthafuckas

involved disappear. And give Slick a warning. I know he's your family but he better not EVER call me again."

"I'll set him straight."

"You do that. Oh, and Mike," I stopped him before he could head to the elevator.

"What's up?" he asked.

"I live here now. Sometimes you might need to come over and discuss business. When you do and Cross is here, I don't need you mean mugging him. Either be cordial or don't even look in his direction...period."

"Look Charly, I got mad love for you and baby girl and if that's your dude I'll respect it. But at the end of the day, my loyalty lies with your father, so his enemies are my enemies."

"I get it but that's Cadence father. You feel me. We don't do disrespect here. Everyone needs to do better. I won't have her torn between two sides. She could care less about loyalty, she cares about the people who love her."

"I feel you and I definitely respect that. Just be careful. Cross may be on the up and up but this father and oldest brother, don't trust them. And that's not your father talking that's me talking," Big Mike emphasized.

"Duly noted." I watched him get on the elevator and leave, before closing the door and going back inside. The warning Big Mike gave me regarding Cross's father and oldest brother didn't move me one way or the other. They had always been on my shit list and being in a relationship with Cross didn't suddenly take them off. I did however appreciate the reminder they were not to be trusted.

Chapter 14

Cross

I was pacing back and forth rubbing my hands together trying to calm my nerves. I don't know why the thought of Charly being with Luca was bothering me so much. It's not like she cheated on me. I wasn't even here but it didn't ease my frustration.

Charly entered the bedroom, interrupting my thoughts. "Babe what's wrong?" she asked closing the door behind her. She walked over to me and placed her hands on my face. "Talk to me, what's wrong?"

"Were you planning on telling me about you and Luca?"

"Is that what you're upset about?" Charly stepped back.

"Hell yeah!" I popped. "That was a stupid ass question. He's my cousin!"

"I know exactly who he is. I don't need you to tell me that." I could see Charly was vexed.

"You should've told me. You got me out here lookin' crazy! I was fuckin blindsided!"

"Are you fuckin' kidding me right now? Nigga, I don't owe you shit! You weren't a part of my life. Do you want to go down the list of my fuck buddies? Get the fuck outta here wit' that bullshit! I'm a grown ass muthafuckin' woman and I don't answer to no nigga that's dickin' me down!" Now it was Charly who was pacing back and forth. "And you gonna step to me wit' some old ass bullshit? Yes I fucked Luca, I fucked him a bunch of damn times, you wanna know how many? How about positions? You wanna know if he eats pussy better than you? What you wanna know."

"Yo, your fuckin' mouth is reckless!" I spit,

pointing my finger at Charly.

"I don't need this shit!" she turned to leave the room but I grabbed her. "Get off of me Cross." Charly attempted to wiggle out of my grasp.

"No, I'm not letting you leave." Charly continued to struggle to get away. I pinned her up against the wall by her throat. "I'm yo' fuckin' man! I'm yo' fuckin man!" I repeated in case it didn't register the first time. "I ain't some nigga dickin' you down! Don't ever let me get blindsided like that again. I've spent all day thinking about killin' that muthafucka!" I could feel the fire in my eyes but Charly had no fear in hers.

Charly touched my face, "He's irrelevant. Baby, do you really think he means anything to me?" I relaxed the grip around her neck. The calmness in her voice soothed the savage beast in me. "Cross, let go of my neck and we can sit down." I did what she asked. Charly took my hand and led me to the bed and we sat down.

"Listen, Luca and I kicked it throughout the years but we're just friends now. I don't want you getting riled up over something that's not important to me. Now you said you're all in and that means we got a shit load of opposition coming from our families but you can't get mad over every man I've ever been with."

"But he ain't every man, Luca's my cousin."

"I get that. Maybe I should've told you but I don't care about Luca like that. I love you," Charly insisted.

"I'm sorry. I kept replaying the night at Francesco's when he kissed you on the cheek and you moved away, or the look on his face when he interrupted our kiss. I'll admit. I'm a jealous man."

"Cross, there's no need to be jealous. I'm all yours and you know that."

"I know but just the thought of you two, then the way I found out."

"How did you find out because I know for damn sure it wasn't from Luca."

"Jr, saw y'all going to a hotel or some shit."

"And just felt the need to tell you huh?" Charly had a suspicious look on her face. "He probably enjoyed dropping that little nugget on you too."

"Of course. I did my best not to let him know but it's been eating me up since I found out."

"Cross, are you sure you really want to do this? I mean really." Charly gave me a serious gaze.

"Yes." I grabbed her hands. "I'm all in. I want to start a life with you. I love you."

"Do you love the idea of me or do you really love me? Can you accept my past, my present and what might happen in the future?"

"I know you had a life before me and you have a life now but I'm all in."

"A few minutes ago did you feel that way."

"Yeah, I did that's why I was gonna kill that nigga Luca. But I overreacted. We all have a past including me." I could see Charly wasn't convinced and I wanted to switch up the sullen mood. "Let's take Tia up on her offer and go out tonight. We can get a hotel suite and come home in the morning."

"Maybe another time. I'm not really in the mood to go out anymore." Charly got up off the bed.

"Where you going?"

"I need a drink." Charly started to walk out the room.

I pulled her back to me and placed her on my lap. "I love you." We stared each other in the eyes.

"I love you too but maybe love isn't enough."

"Don't say that. Are you having second thoughts about us?"

"Honestly I am. I don't do this. I don't let men into my heart like this. But here I am. I decided to follow my heart and the moment I disappoint you, you seem quick to turn on me." Charly got up and walked over by the window.

I followed her and wrapped my arms tightly around her waist. "I handled the situation wrong. I know you had a life while I was away but the Luca thing hit so close to home. But I'll get over it because I want this to work." My lips found their way to the side of Charly's neck. I had to make things right. I let my ego get in the way. "I love you," I whispered in her ear. When Charly didn't reciprocate, it didn't sit right with me.

"I hear you but..."

"But what, Charly?" I released my grip from her and stepped back. "Tell me what you want to do. Do you need time to think about things? I mean, what you wanna do?"

"I need to think." Charly still faced the window and even though I could reach out and touch her, there was definitely a barrier between us.

"Would you prefer I go stay at a hotel? Give you time alone."

Charly finally turned around to face me. "No, that's not gonna fix anything. You leaving because we had an argument isn't the answer."

"Then what is? I can't read minds, Charly. If you want to fix this, then I need to know how you feel," I contended.

Charly walked over and stood in front of me. "I'm scared ok. And I'm not use to being scared and I don't like it. I was never taught how to deal with fear. I'm Charly Brinx but the way I love you, scares me. For so long, I have lived with what ifs, we both have but the what IF, it was supposed to stay like that. I can't live my life in a fairytale. I live in reality and the truth is, we're strangers with a history and a teenage daughter you just found out we share. We've started this relationship with me disappointing you. But I'm human and I know I will disappoint you again. I'm scared that if I disappointment you one too many times, you'll disappear out my life, like you did all those years ago. I dealt with you leaving me then because you were never mine to begin with. But now...getting a taste of how complete my life feels with you in it. I couldn't handle you walking away again. The pain would be too much for me to endure. So yes, I'm scared, Cross."

I stared into Charly's pretty brown eyes and instinctively I knew what I had to do. I got up and walked out the room.

Chapter 15

Charly

"Niggas ain't shit!" I fumed, while making myself something to eat.

I took a pack of ground beef out the refrigerator, threw it in a bowl and added a pack of Lipton onion soup mix to it. After I made the hamburger patties I washed my hands and I took out the lettuce, tomatoes, cheese, and bacon. I was cursing Cross ass out the entire time I was preparing my meal. *I let myself be vulnera-*

ble with a man for the first time and instead of a mutherfucka showing some sensitivity, he leaves the house. Never again! This nigga gon' make me stop fuckin' wit' men altogether, I thought to myself slamming the refrigerator shut.

As soon as the bacon started to crisp, I heard the front door open. "Stay calm Charly, stay calm." I kept my back turned, fighting the urge to throw a knife at Cross ass.

"Charly! "Cross sang my name but I didn't respond. "Charly!" I continued ignoring him while cooking. *This mofo been gone for over two hours and think he can just pop back up, call my name and I'm supposed respond like it's all love. Get the fuck outta here!* "Charly!" This time Cross screamed so loud, everyone in the building including the doorman probably heard him.

I spun around so fast it almost made me dizzy. "What!" I shouted. Cross was standing there with a bouquet of red roses and a big ass grin on his face.

"This is not how I planned it but..." Cross then dropped to one knee. "I let you slip through my fingers once and I won't allow the love of my life slip away again. Charly Brinx, I love all that is you. Your reckless mouth, your spitfire attitude, the way you love our daughter, and your heart. If you say yes to me, I will spend the rest of my life making you the happiest woman in the world. Starting right now. I know you're scared but I'm not. I'll be fearless for the both of us. Baby, will you marry me?" Cross opened a small black velvet box and the glow from the 7 carat emerald cut canary diamond with diamonds cascading down the side of the band made my eyes sparkle.

"Yes! Yes, I'll marry you!" I accepted without hesitation. Cross placed the ring on my finger, then he swept me up in his arms and spun me around.

"I love you, baby! I don't want to wait. We can catch the red eye and go to Vegas. No one has to know. We can do all that formal shit later. What you think?"

"I don't need a big wedding but I want Cadence there and Tia, I need her there too."

"Ok, plan B, we get married here. Tomorrow we go apply for a marriage license."

"Yes! That way Cadence won't have to move around too much. Let's go tell Cadence. I can't wait to see her face."

"Too late I got it all on video." Cadence had been standing there videotaping the entire proposal.

"Cadence!"

"Sorry, Ma. I was just meddling cuz I heard y'all arguing earlier but when I heard Cross come back. When he dropped to his knew, I couldn't resist."

"So you approve?" Cross asked her.

"Yeah, duh! But I think you should go to Vegas. I don't have to be there."

"You don't want to be at our wedding?" I was shocked by Cadence response.

"I mean I just want y'all to get married. I'm not stupid. I know about everything between granddaddy and Cross's father. Ma, don't look like that, I told you the streets be talking."

"You and the damn streets. Cross, the streets be talking." I imitated Cadence. We all laughed.

"But seriously you don't think we should have a small ceremony here?" Cross questioned.

"I'm just saying, why wait?" Cadence shrugged her shoulders.

"And who's gonna stay with you?" I folded my arms waiting to hear the bullshit Cadence was about to throw at us.

"Ma, I'm not a baby, plus Diamond can come stay with me."

"You must think this heavy ring on my finger made me lose my mind...not! It won't be a party over here, no ma'am. Not on my watch." I made clear to Cadence.

"I'm with your mother on this one."

I winked my eye at Cross, letting him know I appreciated him backing me up.

"I'm trying to help y'all out." Cadence smiled.

"We good over here but thanks." I told her. "Nice try though."

"All I'm saying is I think it would be pretty cool if you all went to Vegas and got married. We would be like a legit family. However you decide to do it, is fine with me," Cadence beamed giving me and Cross a hug before going back upstairs.

"Fuck it! Let's go to Vegas tonight!" I cheered.

"Are you serious?" Cross wanted to confirm.

"Yes! Let's make those flight arrangements before I change my mind."

"But what about you wanting Tia to be there. Cadence made it pretty clear she didn't care." Cross laughed.

"I know right! It's last minute but let me call Tia now," I said grabbing my cell.

"Who can that be?" Cross wondered out

loud after hearing the doorbell ring. "You get Tia on the phone, I'll get the door."

"Perfect!"

"No need to make that call," Cross said, quickly returning with Santi and Tia following behind him.

"Damn y'all doing it right! Santi said noticing the bottle of champagne and bottle of Hennessey."

"Great timing! We was about to pour us some drinks. You can join us," I said getting two more glasses from the cabinet.

"What's the occasion?" Tia asked sitting down at the table.

I turned around and flashed my hand.

"Holy shit!" Tia screamed as she almost trampled me. "Bitch, why you didn't tell me!"

"It just happened not too long ago."

"Girl, I'm so happy for you!" Tia hugged me. "Yasssssss bitch, yassssss!" Tia grabbed her glass. "Girl we gotta clink, clink to this!" Tia's excitement was contagious.

And suddenly it hit me, ohmigoodness I'm getting married. I wanted to call my daddy but shook that thought out my head.

"Cross, you the man! That ring is gorgeous!

Well done!" Tia praised, pouring everyone a drink.

"Well you know, I try." Cross smiled widely.

"Shit, Cross you put the sun on her damn finger." Santi admired the ring. "So when's the big day?"

Cross and I looked at each other. "That's the dilemma. We want to go to Vegas tonight but we can't leave Cadence and Charly wants Tia at her side."

"Awww bestie!" Tia hit my arm. "I know you love me." She teased.

"We thought about waiting until this weekend and just getting married here with just you guys."

"Nah, let's go to Vegas! What about Miss Erma? Cadence can stay with your daddy."

"Yeah, telling daddy would be a great idea." I hissed, in a sarcastic tone.

"I didn't say tell him. I said let Cadence stay with him."

"Tia has a point. what you think, Charly?" Cross asked.

"Sounds like a plan to me!" I snatched up my phone and walked into the living room to call Miss Erma.

"Hey, Miss Erma."

"Hey, baby girl!"

"I know it's last minute but can Cadence stay over there? I'm going out of town for a couple days and Tia can't watch her."

"That's fine. Your father actually had to go out of town too and I don't like being here alone. Better yet, I'll come over there. Cadence doesn't need to be moving around like that."

"That's perfect! Thank you so much, Miss Erma."

"My pleasure. See you soon!"

I ended the call and went back in the kitchen to share the good news.

"What she say?" Tia asked.

"It's on and poppin'! She said she'll come over here so Cadence doesn't have to move around too much."

"That's even better." Cross said, staring at his phone. "They have a flight leaving in three hours. So, we gonna do this?" he stared up at me.

"Let's do it." I smiled.

"Shit, I'm going too." Santi said. "Y'all niggas didn't invite me but I'm going."

"Nigga, you're my brother, you know you're going with us." Cross mugged Santi.

"Y'all so cute but we got a lot of packing to do. We need to hurry this up, if we gon' make that flight." Tia told us.

"What we need to pack for? We can buy what we need when we get there." Santi responded.

"I'm wit' Santi, we can go shopping when we get to Vegas," Cross cosigned. "Here put your info in, so I can book the flight." Cross handed Santiago the phone and he passed it to Tia when he finished.

"Yassssss first class. You alright with me Cross." Tia danced in her seat. She handed me the phone and I added my information and gave it back to Cross.

"A'ight it's booked." Cross announced. "I also got us a penthouse suite with fountain views. I want the best for my baby and my fam," he said smiling at Santi and Tia.

"Yes!" Tia screamed. "You're getting married, bitch!" Tia started singing and dancing around kitchen.

Of course I had to join in. "I'm getting married........."

Chapter 16

Cross

Charly and I held hands as we snuggled in the seat. Tia and Santi were in the seats across from us looking more like a couple then fuck buddies. "Hmmmm, it seems like my brother might be feeling Tia," I commented to Charly.

"Yeah, I noticed that too. They're holding hands like us. Maybe we'll see wedding bells in their future too," Charly smiled.

"Slow down. Not sure Santi ready to trade

in his player ways for monogamy just yet."

"You never know. I told you he met his match with Tia. From the looks of things, I was right."

"Can't disagree with you about that. Santi ain't never been the public affectionate type but Tia seems to bring out his affectionate side. This might be the real deal."

"I think it is."

"I know we're the real deal," I said, kissing Charly on the lips. "In a few hours we'll no longer be boyfriend/girlfriend. We'll be husband and wife. Are you nervous?"

Charly looked up at me. "Nope. I'm not nervous at all. I'm excited."

"Me too. It's long overdue." We kissed again before Charly closed her eyes to get some sleep for the duration of our flight. Instead of me resting, my thoughts drifted back to everything that had taken place, to finally get us to this moment, starting with my ex-wife.

The truth was, my marriage to Tiffany was fucked up from the get go. My heart was always with Charly, even when I wasn't ready to admit it to myself. I remember one of the last arguments Tiffany and I had before I knew the marriage was done. She made a comment that she felt like she was chasing a ghost. Like she was competing with someone who wasn't even there. I figured it was her paranoia because Tiffany knew I was cheating but couldn't prove it. So, I brushed her off and called her crazy but that wasn't the truth. I went through the motions but my heart was always someplace else. I overcompensated with material things. Making sure she had everything and anything she wanted, except what Tiffany wanted the most...my heart.

There was a disconnect there, that no amount of money, jewelry or gifts could fix. I remember the day it all came full circle and exploded in both of our faces. I came home early from work to shower, so I could meet up with one of my numerous side chicks. The multiple women I was seeing, were more like stress relievers than anything else. When I walked into the house, I noticed a pair of Jordan's by the door and I knew they weren't mine. I scanned the room and nothing else was noticeably out of place. But there was a faint smell of weed and air freshener that filled my nose. As I made my way through the house, Tiffany's moans could be heard coming from our bedroom. The door was ajar and when I walked in the room, there she was, legs wrapped around a nigga's back, as he was dicking her down. There was no anger or rage, I felt relief. This was my out. The only thing that rubbed me the wrong way, was I couldn't stand a disrespectful motherfucker. To fuck another nigga in my bed and my house, that I pay the bills at, was unacceptable. I should've tossed her trifling ass out the window for that shit alone but I was so happy to be rid of her without guilt, I let it slide.

I cleared my throat and scared the shit out of them. Tiffany tried to explain herself while the nigga, who was no more than twenty-one max, scrambled to his feet to gather his clothes. He must've thought I was gonna try to fight him or something but I didn't say a word. Honestly, I wanted to thank him for giving me a justifiable reason to exit a loveless marriage. If Tiffany had continued to play the role of a dutiful wife and mother, we would still be married now. It wasn't like she was stopping me from doing what the fuck I wanted to do. But a chick, who was bringing nothing to the table but her pussy, wasn't about to be fuckin' another nigga in my house, on my dime. Nah, that's where I draw the line.

As I maneuvered around the room packing my belongings, I ignored Tiffany's cries and pleas. At one point, she latched onto my leg and was dragged all the way to the front door. She just wouldn't let go. As I stepped over the threshold, Tiffany finally loosened her grip and I was able to shake her off. Seeing her lay in the doorway of what used to be our home, I put the car in reverse and backed out of the driveway. I never stepped foot in that house again.

Charly's grip tightened in her sleep as we hit a little turbulence but she never woke up. I had been lost in my own thoughts and didn't realize she was still laying on my chest. I watched her resting peacefully for a few minutes and a smile crept across my face. With all the bullshit I went through with Tiffany, I wouldn't change a thing. We share three beautiful kids and more importantly, it prepared me for this moment right here. Never take love for granted and finding your soulmate was truly a blessing.

"Yo, this fuckin' place is sweet!" Santi bellowed, when we got to the room. Santi and I were in one penthouse suite while Charly and Tia were in the other. Charly didn't want me to see her all dolled up until the wedding, even though I personally picked out the dress she was wearing. I thought it was so cute though, especially since she's more gun toting gangster then a sentimental girly girl.

"Yeah, it looks even better than the images online," I commented, sitting down across from Santi who wasted no time raiding the mini bar.

"Here, have a drink." Santi passed me one of the liquor bottles.

"Let me stay sober until after the wedding. I wanna be in my right mind when Charly and I exchange vows."

"I feel you," Santi chuckled, opening another bottle.

"I noticed you didn't answer my question about Tia."

"What question?"

"Oh, you forgot that quick," I cracked. "When we were on the elevator, I said you met your match with Tia didn't you?" I laughed, opening a bottled water.

"Man, she got that voodoo pussy! But it's more than that, she's a cool chick. By now, I would've found a reason to fall back. You know how I do but she's different. Tia has her shit together and she's smart."

"I never thought I would see the day, you'd be feeling a female. Whatever happens, don't do no foul shit. Tia is Charly's ride or die. If you fuck her over, I'll never hear the end of it."

"Cross, I got you. I won't fuck this up. I'm feelin' Tia. She's good people. Now let me ask you a question."

"Go for it."

"How did you know Charly was the one?"

"She's always been the one. That night all those years ago, it's like we connected on a level much deeper than just great sex. I wanna say I regret I didn't try harder to reconnect with Charly but then, I wouldn't have my three kids with Tiffany and you know how much I love them. I gotta believe it all worked out the way it was supposed to, or I wouldn't be able to deal with the guilt."

"You making up for it now and I respect that. Everybody isn't gonna be thrilled for you but I am. You were never happy in your marriage. I could see it. Even on your wedding day, you didn't look at Tiffany the way you look at Charly."

"Wow, you could tell?"

"Yeah. I don't know if anybody else noticed but I did."

"It's always been about Charly. I chased her in my dreams but..."

"Now it's a reality."

"Damn right!"

Santi looked around and then jumped up. "This suite is the fuckin' business! Shit, could you imagine living here?"

"Nah, I like my surroundings to be peaceful. I couldn't live Vegas. This place is always on ten. Never any down time."

"You're so different from us. Curtis Jr. would've been screaming from the balcony by now, probably naked."

"True," I laughed. "Speaking of him, we gotta plan a going away party."

"I have an even better idea," Santi jumped in and said.

"I'm listening."

"How about a coming out party for you and Charly and a going away party for Curtis Jr. We can combine the two. It'll also be a way to get both the families together," Santi suggested.

"Man, I don't know. I highly doubt Charly will go for it."

"Cross, you can be very persuasive when you wanna be. It's hard for people to tell you no."

"I'll think about it," I said, raising up off the sofa. "Come on best man. Let's get ready for this wedding. I'm about to be a married man!" I announced unable to contain my enthusiasm.

Chapter 17

Charly

"I'm done with the makeup, now it's time for me to do your hair!" Tia exclaimed, plugging in the flat iron she bought when we first got here.

"That's not necessary. Cross likes my hair natural. He thinks it's sexy, so I'm going to wear it curly for our wedding."

"Aww that's so cute! Cross has really changed you. Now I know you're still a cold hearted bitch and all but there's a softness about you now. It's so enduring and cute! And it's all due to Cross."

"Hush!" I playfully slapped Tia on the arm. Truth is, Tia was right. Cross has a quiet strength about him that allows me to just feel like his woman.

"You know I'm right!" Tia nudged me.

"You are," I unwillingly agreed. "I'm still getting used to this hold Cross has over me. Dare I say, I'm a tad bit scared."

"Love can be scary but it's okay. I think your dad has convinced you that you gotta be hard all the time, no boo, you're a woman first and foremost, who just happens to be a Queenpin that kills mufuckas in a blink of an eye." Tia joked but was dead ass serious. "Real talk, I don't care how strong you are, a woman needs a safe place to fall. And Cross is your safe place."

"Well, since you all up in my feelings what's the word on you and Santi? I know you feeling that nigga."

Tia tilted her head to the side, "I am. He's fun, exciting and dangerous. All the traits I love in a man," she giggled.

"Yeah, yeah, yeah you already told me that but what's beneath the surface?"

"Fine! He's thoughtful, he listens, and we talk as much as we fuck."

I made a face.

"No, I'm serious we do. He's really interested in what I'm doing with my business. He thinks I'm amazing you know." Tia laughed "But we talk! Like deep serious conversations. And baby when I tell you the dick, oh the dick is so good. Maybe too good," she sulked.

"Is that even possible?"

"Technically, no. But when the dick is too good, a nigga will have you out here slippin'. I know Santi is a player and I don't wanna get played...you feel me."

"Girl, you in love wit' that nigga!" my mouth dropped open. "I'm happy for you, Tia." I stood up and hugged her.

"I didn't mean for it to happen but it did," Tia said nervously. "Now my ass is scared just like you," she threw her hands up.

"You don't have anything to worry about. You got Santi open. You never know the next wedding might be yours!" I winked. "Now let me go put on my dress. I don't want to keep my soon to be husband waiting any longer."

When we arrived at the chapel, I wasn't expecting such a beautiful venue. With the wedding being planned so last minute, I didn't have high expectations but like always, Cross delivered. There were three elegant wedding chapels as well as a an outdoor gazebo and glass garden. The cobblestone accented grounds with lush landscaping made you feel like you were in a botanical garden paradise. The backdrop for us to exchange I do's was a cascading waterfall and a lagoon.

The dress I was wearing was perfect for the whole beachy feel of our wedding. It now made sense why Cross chose it. When I began slowly walking down the rose petal isle, I could see the lust and love in Cross's eyes. The beautiful silk bodice with artfully hand cut lace and drapes of chiffon flowing against the thigh high slits, accessorized with diamond stud earrings and a three row V-shape diamond choker necklace, had me feeling like a sexy princess.

"You look amazing." Cross's eyes danced all around my body. "You ready to do this?"

"Yes," I beamed.

Before we exchanged vows, Cross wanted to say what he described as an expression of his love. I began to tear up, although he hadn't spoken one word yet. I blamed it on having an emotional high.

"When you find a woman who makes it hard for you to breathe when she walks in the room because she takes your breath away, she's the one. If she makes your heart beat faster when you're around her, she's the one. You have always been the one for me Charly Brinx. I want to be the King you need because you are my true Queen." Cross put his hand out for me to take. I placed my hand in his and together we knew this was our destiny.

"Mrs. Cross Payne," Cross grinned as he carried me into our hotel suite. When we went into our bedroom the concierge had the middle of the bed decorated with red rose petals in a prefect shaped heart. There was also a bottle of expensive champagne chilling in the bucket but who had time to drink bubbly, when we were already undressing each other.

"Baby, you feel so damn good," Cross moaned in my ear when our bodies became one. There was this warmth we generated between each other. I closed my eyes and got lost as Cross slow dragged inside me. He kept his rhythm steady and as he went deeper into my sugar walls, I gazed up at him and our eyes locked. It was these moments when we connected on a more profound level. His eyes told me he loved me and my eyes told Cross, I loved him more than life itself. Once our eyes finished communicating, my husband released everything he had inside of me. If I wasn't already pregnant, then we definitely made a baby tonight.

"Back to the real world we go," I sighed, grabbing my purse.

"You sound sad, baby. You wanna stay another day?" Cross asked placing his arm around my waist.

"Say yes! Say yes!" Tia cheered while sitting on Santi's lap. "I'm loving Vegas. Aren't you, babe?" she asked kissing Santi.

"You already know I fucks wit' this city!" Santi chimed in."

"Mrs. Payne, the choice is yours."

I blushed every time Cross called me that.

"I would love to stay an extra day but I really want to check on Cadence and I need to make sure business is running properly, before my dad decides to replace me."

"Girl, your daddy ain't gon' ever replace you," Tia grunted. "But I know you're a workaholic so I understand you wanting to get back to business. Speaking of business, have you gotten any leads on who tried to kill us?" Tia asked.

"Hell no!" I eyed Cross. Both of us had become frustrated over the situation.

"Baby, I'm working on it," Cross tried to assure me. "But my men haven't been able to come up with anything. The streets have even gone silent. It's like the shooters vanished into thin air. Normally, someone would be running they mouth by now but nada."

"It be like that sometime," Santi shrugged. "In the line of work our families are in, shit like this happen."

"Not to fuckin' me!" I belted. "Them mutha-fuckas came to my crib where my child lives.

What if she had been walking out with me and Tia. Or would've Cross never showed up!" I was now screaming at the top of my lungs becoming irate.

"Charly, baby calm down. We had this wonderful trip. Let's not ruin it." Cross had me in a close embrace. He lifted my chin and stared down at me like only he could.

"Don't try to hypnotize me with those jet black eyes," I gushed.

"I tell ya'll what. We catch our flight today but I'll make reservations for us to come back in a couple weeks. How's that sound?" Cross asked us. "Everybody who's down raise their hands." All hands rose up immediately.

"Once again, you managed to make me feel like everything will be fine," I said, stroking Cross's face.

"Because it will. This right here, this thing between us. We have to keep it sacred, untouched. We can't let the outside world penetrate the love we have for each other. We'll constantly have obstacles thrown our way but as long as you and I are one, we'll come out on top...always."

"You promise?"

"Charly, how can I not promise when your

voice sounds like the sweet girl I grew up with. I really do bring out the softer side of you."

"Yes and I love you for it. Now let's go home!"

Chapter 18

Cross

"Cross, thanks again for a fuckin' amazing trip. Can't wait for us to do this shit again," Santi grinned when I dropped him and Tia off at her place.

"You really were a great host, Cross. Thanks for letting us tag along for the ride," Tia added.

"Girl, you know I wouldn't go get married without my bestie by my side." Charly got out the car and hugged Tia. "So, what ya' about to get into besides each other," Charly teased.

"We're gonna keep the celebration going and hittin' up that new bar downtown. Isn't that right, Santi?" Tia winked.

"You know how we do. The party don't never stop!" Santi boasted.

"You two lovebirds are welcome to join us but I'm sure the newlyweds want some alone time," Tia said, tugging on Charly's arm.

"I do wanna lay up under my husband, at least for the night, before it's back to business as usual. But let's do lunch later this week, girly."

"For sure!"

"Have fun tonight but ya bet not get in no trouble!" Charly warned, giggling.

"We won't. Pinky promise!" Tia gave Charly one last hug and they exchanged I love you's before she got back in the car.

"Yeah! What my wife said!" I waved, driving away.

"You really did plan the most magnificent trip for our wedding," Charly said, leaning across and resting her head on my shoulder. "The only thing missing was the rest of our family."

"Our father's not accepting us being together is really bothering you isn't it?"

"I had this middle finger us against them attitude and for a minute it was real. But my father was the first man I ever loved and besides you...the only. Embarking on this new journey of my life without him being a part of it, is disheartening."

"Can I just say, I'm so proud of you, Charly. Proud to call you my wife."

"Where is this coming from you?"

"Lately, you've been revealing this other side of yourself, being vulnerable without fear. That's what you call true bravery. For a long time, I didn't even think that was a possibility for you but I was wrong."

"Stop making me blush." Charly punched me in the arm. "But seriously, you make it easy for me to let down my guard because I know you love me unconditionally."

"I really do," I said stopping the car in front of the entrance of our building. "Baby, I hope you don't mind but I really wanna stop by my parent's house so I can check on my mom. Curtis Jr. sent me a text saying she wasn't doing too well."

"Of course. Go be with Miss Lita. Take your time. I'll be here waiting for you."

"Thanks, babe. I'll make it up to you tonight."
I leaned over and put my tongue down Charly's
throat, so she would know what to look forward
to when I got home."

I was having a pleasant visit with my mother
but my Pops couldn't let me make my exit in
peace. He got wind I went to Vegas with Charly
and flipped out. The crazy part is, he didn't even
know we got married, he just felt I was neglecting
business and our family. I tried my best to ignore
his foolishness but he persisted.

"Pops! You buggin' out! I'm not neglecting
business or this family. Don't you see I'm here
to spend time with my mother. Did it occur to
you, I needed to take a step back, to escape all
this negativity you suffocating me with. Ain't
but so much of this unnecessary cynicism I can
take," I scoffed. "Maybe it's cool with you, but
it's time I put me and my family's needs first for
a change!"

"We ARE your family, Croccifixio! We
ARE!!!" Pop screamed as he hit his chest. "Not
some little bitch you done fell in love with."

Something in me snapped and I was standing face to face with my father. "Don't you EVER disrespect Charly like that? EVER!"

"You stepping to me boy?!" Pops eyes were full of rage. For a split second I thought I saw murder in his eyes.

"You damn right!" I hated disrespecting my father but he pushed me too far.

"Get the hell out my house!" He was so furious, spit was flying from his mouth. A degree of fury came across his face I had never seen before inside the house. On the streets yeah, it was that look he had before he killed someone. Never did I believe my own father would be directing the glare of death at me.

"You ain't said nothing but a word." I stormed off his estate without looking back. During the drive home I was fuming. There was no way I could tell Charly about this. She would never forgive him, hell I may never forgive him. I could see why him and Charlie Brinx were best friends, they had to be two of the oldest most stubborn assholes breathing.

Right when I thought my night couldn't get no more fucked up, I noticed my ex-wife Tiffany calling. I wanted to hit decline but she could've been calling about our kids and I didn't want to chance it.

"Hello."

"Is it true you got fuckin' married?!" Tiffany screamed in the phone.

"Who told you that?"

"That daughter of yours posted pics on Instagram and Kayla follows her. So of course she saw the shit," Tiffany smacked.

"Her name is Cadence," I said, checkin' Tiffany. "I meant to tell the kids before they heard it from someone else. I apologize. Cadence probably thought they already knew. She meant no harm."

"I guess that's your polite way of saying you did marry that chick. How the fuck you marry another woman and not tell me."

"Tiffany, I ain't got to tell you shit! You my ex-wife for a reason."

"Then explain how the hell you run off and marry a woman your kids have never even met?! You the same selfish bastard you've always been," she huffed. "From what I hear, yo' daddy don't even like that hoe. Let's see how long this quickie marriage of yours last!" Tiffany spit.

"Mind yo' business, Tiffany and keep my

wife's name out your mouth. I'll make this right with my kids. But if you try to poison them against me, all that extra money I give you in spousal support, will go right out the fuckin' window," I threatened before ending the call.

Chapter 19

Charly

"I knew you were going to fall asleep." Cross said, when he came in the bedroom.

"I was doing my best to wait up for you," I mumbled. "How did everything go with your mom?" I asked lifting my head up.

"It was straight until my Pops had to make his presence known. But I don't wanna talk about him right now. I'm exhausted."

"I hope not too exhausted for me." I bit down

on my lip watching my husband strip down. Damn he was fine and he was all mine. My eyes stared at his third leg that was semi erect.

"Stop staring at my dick." Cross said, climbing in bed behind me. I scooted up as we both got adjusted. I laid my head back on his firm chest.

"I can't help myself. You woke me up, now you have to put me back to sleep."

"What type of husband would I be, if I deny my new bride." Cross kissed my earlobe then played with my nipples with his fingers, they we're getting harder by the minute. I moaned softly as Cross's hands roamed my body. His touch was tantalizing me and although I was tired, every part of my body perked up. The softness of his lips as he kissed me made me cry out to have him inside of me.

I turned to face him, then I crawled up his muscular statuesque body like he was my prey. As I lowered myself down on his massive golden rod my insides felt tender and I winced in pain.

"Baby, you ok?"

"Yeah, I'm just a little sensitive but I got it." I gyrated around until my love juices started to flow. I stared Cross deep in his eyes and I took the dick. I took him by surprise the way I balanced myself and went all the way down and all the way back up on his rock hard tool. When the tip of his head hit the rim of my pussy, the sensation was amazing. I couldn't help but scream his name.

"Oh shit Charly!" I now had Cross calling my name and listening to him beg for more, made me work it even harder. Cross's eyes were rolling to the back of his head. Watching him cum with such intensity, did something to me. It made me want my husband even more. I collapsed into his strong arms and we fell into a serene sleep.

Ring...Ring...Ring...

I started tossing and turning in my sleep, thinking I was having some sort of bizzare dream where a phone was ringing. I moved closer to Cross and put a pillow over my head, hoping it would make the ringing stop but it didn't, it continued.

When I opened my eyes, I realized it was the home phone. "Who the hell could be calling this late," I muttered reaching for the phone. "Hello."

I went from halfway sleep to wide awake in a matter of seconds. I dropped the phone and my ear piercing screams woke Cross up.

"What the fuck!" Cross instinctively reached for his gun, jumped out of bed aiming towards the door. Making sure he hit his mark, he flipped on the light switch. But instead of discovering an intruder, he saw me bawling my eyes out. "Baby, what's wrong?" Cross kneeled down on the floor next to me.

I was hyperventilating. I could hardly breathe let alone talk. After consoling me for a few minutes, I was finally able to stutter a few words.

"Tia, is dead," I managed to say before breaking down and sobbing hysterically all over again. I saw Cross pick up the phone I dropped and he started talking to the person on the other end. He knew that was the only way he could get answers because I was too distraught. I guess after getting all the details, he finally hung up.

"Damn." Cross slumped down in the chair and put his head down. "I can't believe Tia is dead." For the duration of the night he held me tightly as I cried my heart out.

Two Weeks Later...

"Santi, how you holding up? I haven't seen you since Tia's funeral." I asked when I came downstairs and saw him in the kitchen speaking with Cross.

"Not good. I don't think I've accepted she's really gone."

"I know what you mean. I keep calling her phone thinking she's gonna answer and be like what's up bitch, let's go shopping." My voice trembled and I stopped myself from crying.

"It's okay, baby." Cross held me.

"No it's not. How could she have been so reckless," I shouted angrily. "I always used to joke with Tia about being a lush and drinking too much but to be out late at night, drinking while it's pouring down rain. For goodness sake, they found an open bottle of wine in her car! I still can't believe her car went over that bridge," I cried.

"This whole situation is sad. It made me

rethink how I conduct myself on occasion. I've gotten behind the wheel of the car drunk plenty of times. Only by luck and the Grace Of God, did I make it to my destination safely without killing myself or someone else. I'm done with that shit." Cross was adamant.

"What I'll never know is why she was calling me late that night. Then she sent me a text saying she was on her way over. It will always haunt me that Tia might've been rushing to come see me when she went over that bridge, "I sniveled.

"I know why Tia was on her way over to see you," Santi looked up at me and said.

"Why?" Cross questioned before I could.

"We had went out partying that night. We were both on a romantic high from our Vegas trip. When we got back to her place, I asked Tia to marry me and she said yes."

"What!" Cross and I both blurted out at the same time.

"Yeah," Santi nodded somberly. "Curtis Jr. called me and said I needed to come to Pop's house. If I had stayed with Tia that night, she would've never been out." He shook his head.

"You can't blame yourself. Tia was head strong like me, plus she was a free spirit. It wouldn't have mattered what time of the night it was, if she wanted to come over, nobody could've stopped her."

"Maybe, but at least I probably would've been driving and Tia wouldn't be dead right now."

"Both of you," Cross said, staring at me and Santi. "Stop doing this to yourselves. Tia wouldn't want this. She had a big heart and was full of life. What happened was a tragic accident and we can all learn something from it."

"Baby, you're right. Tia wouldn't want us playing the blame game. I'm just happy my girl found true love before she died. She was really crazy about you, Santi and it's good to know you loved her too."

"I did. Tia was amazing. I don't think I'll ever find another woman like her." Santi's eyes watered up. Cross walked over and patted his brother on the shoulder. We were all feeling the loss of my best friend and none of our lives would ever be the same again.

Chapter 20

Cross

When I left the house, the movers were packing up the few things Charly insisted on bringing to the new house. She had found a six bedroom seven bath mansion on the outskirts of the city. Charly fell in love with the home the moment she opened the door and entered the foyer. And what Charly wants Charly gets. My daughter Kayla was visiting, she and Cadence both loved it too. It really didn't matter to me, as long as my wife was happy.

Charly had been on an emotional roller-coaster since Tia's death. With us moving into our new home and Kayla being here, it really kept Charly busy and helped her from falling into a deep depression. I'd been worried about her mental health but being the warrior she is, my wife pushed through. Her strength made me want to go out my way to bring some peace to her life.

"I'm surprised to see you here," Pops commented, continuing to read through some papers on his desk without looking up at me. I knew he wanted to make me feel small, so I would be pissed off and leave. But I was willing to be at his mercy for Charly.

"I came here to ask for your forgiveness. The last time I was here, I let my temper get the best of me. You're my father and I should always show you the utmost respect."

My father was clearly impressed with my attempt at a cease-fire because he dropped his pen and his eyes met mine. "I wondered how long it would take for you to come around and acknowledge your mistake. It takes a real man to admit when they're wrong."

"Then I'm assuming you're willing to

concede to your missteps also." I countered.

"I thought this apology was about you," Pops said, getting up from his chair and pouring himself some scotch.

"It's about us and our family. I'm not sure if you heard but Charly and I got married." My father almost dropped his glass on the hardwood floor, so I knew that meant the information hadn't reached him yet.

"Son, I see you're determined to leave me speechless. I would say why her but then I know you. There has to be something special about Charly Brinx. if you chose to make her your wife."

"Is that your attempt at making an effort," I shrugged, determined to remain committed to the reason I was here. "Pops, I love you and respect you. You've always instilled in us the importance of family. Charly is my wife which makes her family. I'm asking you as your son and a man to help put an end to this vendetta between the Payne's and the Brinx family."

"You asking me to choose Charlie Brinx over my own self-respect," Pops mocked, pouring himself another drink.

"No, I'm asking you to choose me. I've spent

my entire life trying to make you proud. I even came home for you. I'm now asking you to do something for me as your son."

Pops let out a long sigh. "What did Charlie say? Did that stubborn sonofabitch agree to put an end to our feud?"

"I haven't spoken to him yet but I did speak to Francesco. He agreed to attend a family event Santi and I are putting together."

"What sort of event?"

"To properly announce my marriage to Charly and a going away party for Curtis Jr."

"How the fuck you get Francesco to agree to come to that?" Pops questioned, leaning back in his chair.

"I'm able to be persuasive when need be."

"You really do love that girl," my Pops stated, as if it was finally registering in his thick skull. "Son, I'll tell you what. I'll attend this gathering but I can't make any promises regarding Charlie Brinx. Take it or leave it."

"I'll take it. But Pops, I'm begging you to make an effort. Charly is my wife and the mother of your granddaughter. If you shut her out, you'll be shutting me out too. I don't want that. I love you. You don't have to respond right now but please think about what I said."

"What's all this?" I asked when I returned home. I noticed a gift box in the middle of the bed.

Charly nervously sat on the bed swinging her legs like a little kid then jumped to her feet.

I looked at her suspiciously. "What are you doing?"

"Nothing." She said in a high pitched voice.

"Mm mhmm." I closed the door behind me.

"Baby, I have something for you." Charly kissed me on my lips before covering my eyes with her hands. "Don't peek either."

"You 'bout to do some freaky shit huh?" I chuckled.

She guided me to the bed and sat me down. "Put your hands out." I follow Charly's request, puzzled yet intrigued by what she had planned. "Okay open your eyes."

The gift box I'd seen on the bed had now been placed in the palm of my hands. I raised an eyebrow. "Hmmm a gift box? What you fit in here?"

"Just open it!"

"Babe, don't play with me." I started shaking my head when I saw three pregnancy test laying side by side. My eyes widened and I was flooded with disbelief. "Are you serious?"

"Dead ass!" Charly smiled.

I jumped to my feet, swooped up my wife up and spun her around. I kissed Charly over and over again before placing her back down. "Baby you having my baby!" I dropped to my knees and placed my head against her stomach like I was listening for a heartbeat.

Charly rubbed my head. "I guess this means you're happy."

I stared up at Charly, mesmerized at how she was even more beautiful to me now. "Baby, you are my happiness."

Chapter 21

Charly

"It's so good to see you, baby!" Miss Erma beamed, when she opened the door and hugged me.

"It's good to see you too. With us moving into the new house and juggling business, it hasn't left me much time to come visit."

"'I understand. You're a family woman now. I'm happy for you. That young man has put a spark in your eyes I have never seen before. You know I love you but there was a coldness there, that I'm sure your daddy instilled in you. That's great for your line of work but you have let that life consume you. You have a right to be happy."

"Thank you Miss Erma."

"Mama Erma....." She reminded me.

"Yes, Mama Erma," I smiled sweetly. She hugged me again with tears in her eyes.

"You don't know how long I have waited to hear you say that."

"You know I love you."

"Yes but it sure feels good to hear it. Yeah, I like this Cross. I look forward to getting to know him. Your daddy and I are going to have a long talk. Don't worry I haven't mentioned the marriage, that's not my place to tell him but he needs a reality check."

"Thank you. We need all the support we can get to bring daddy around. You're more than aware of how set in his ways he can be.

"True...true...true," Mama Erma nodded, looking me up and down.

"What?" I lowered my head trying to figure out why she was looking at me like that.

"Baby girl, are you pregnant?" she whispered.

A look of shock came across my face. "How did you know?"

"You are glowing." She touched my cheeks. "Now that's black girl magic at its finest. Does Cross know?"

"Yeah, we both found out last night."

"You know I know you, so I'm just going to say this, enjoy the journey. You're a thinker. You over analyze everything. Just be happy. You have a lot on your plate, pregnancy, a new marriage, his children are now your children. That's a lot but you're a strong woman and even though you aren't all affectionate, you love hard and the people you love know it. I also realize, not having Tia here to share it all with, is breaking your heart because it's breaking mine too."

"If we have a daughter, I was thinking about naming her after Tia. She would've been such an amazing Auntie. Remember how great she was with Cadence."

"Yes, she I do. We all miss Tia terribly. But don't forget, Tia lives on right here," Mama Erma put her hand to my heart.

"You're absolutely right. I wasn't expecting you to be here when I came but I'm glad you were. I needed this talk. But now it's time for me to face my dad. I came over to tell daddy the truth about my marriage and pregnancy," I said, placing my hand over my stomach.

"Good girl!" Mama Erma smiled proudly. "You got this, Charly."

"We shall see."

Daddy was in the den sitting in his favorite chair when I walked in the room. "Well if it ain't my namesake. I was beginning to wonder if I still had a daughter."

"I'm sorry, Daddy. I should've come to see you but honestly, I didn't think you were all that interested in seeing me."

"I'll admit, I've been hard on you lately. Maybe once you come to your senses and get rid of that Payne boy, things can go back to normal around here."

"Daddy, I hate to break it to you but this is the new normal."

"Ain't nothing normal about you shacking up with Cross Payne." Daddy flung his hand up dismissing what I said.

I was too tired to try and convince my father of anything, so I got straight to the point. "It's way past shacking up. Cross and I got married and I'm pregnant with his child."

"Hell! At least he made an honest woman outta you," daddy sighed. "You determined to make me accept that boy but it ain't gon' happen."

"I think we all know, can't nobody make Charlie Brinx do anything he doesn't want. I want you to be a part of my life and this baby growing inside me but it only can happen, if you can respect Cross as my husband. I can't force you, Daddy but it sure would mean the world to me." I choked up doing my best to fight away the tears but I didn't win the battle.

"Gone over there and get you some tissue. We don't cry in this house...you know that." My dad was doing his best not to meet my gaze. He played hard but I could see my words were chipping away at his tough as nails façade.

"I have to go now, Daddy but next Friday night, we're having a family get together at the Mirage downtown. I would love for you and Mama Erma to attend. If I don't see you, just know I love you and that will never change." I kissed my father on the forehead and quickly rushed out the door before I had a complete meltdown.

"Did I tell you how stunning you look tonight?" Cross glided his hand down my backless red dress, until resting it around my waist.

"Yes, you did my love and you look pretty handsome yourself but that's a given. Maybe I'm bias but I think I have the sexiest husband in the world," I gushed.

"I feel the same way about you. Now let's show our faces at this party, since we are the guests of honor. Then roll out because I'm already anxious to get you home and out this dress," Cross flirted, gripping a handful of my ass.

When we entered, I was impressed at how elegant the venue looked. "Santi, went all out. It's decorated beautifully." I couldn't help but compliment. "I mean, I'm sure he hired someone but whatever event planning company he used did a remarkable job."

"I agree. Very impressive."

Cross and I both admired the modern and glamourous lounge with Swarovski crystal walls that lit up, creating sparkling curtains.

Chairs were upholstered in animal print, while the floors were done in shiny black quartz embedded with crystal dust. The champagne was also flowing but of course that was off limits to me. The place was filled to capacity and it was nice to see so many familiar faces.

"My favorite brother and beautiful sister in law have finally arrived. The party has now officially started!" Santi cheered, greeting us with a drink in both hands. "Come take a picture," he said leading us across the room to a professional photographer he hired for the event. Santi definitely made sure he had everything covered.

As we made our way through the crowd, I peeped the stares and glares we got but Cross was oblivious. He kept kissing me like we were the only ones in the room. I guess it was one thing for people to hear that the son and the daughter of well-known mortal enemies, were now a married couple and to actually see it in person. Because all eyes were locked on our every move.

"Damn smart guy get a room!" Curtis Jr. shouted, when Cross kept putting his hands and lips all over me.

"We already christened all the rooms in our

brand new mansion," Cross bragged to his big brother and I was here for the petty jab since Curtis Jr. was on my shit list about that Luca bullshit.

"Yeah, Cross and Charly doing big thangs!" Santi continued the boasting.

"Oh, you been over there?" Curtis Jr. asked as he shot a look at Cross and me.

"You catch that?" I whispered through a forced smile.

"Yep. Just smile baby."

"I am!"

I faked smiled through what seemed like an endless amount of flashes. When one picture was done being taken, it seemed like someone else was waiting to pose for the camera with us. Cross was taking great pride in introducing me to his family. Everyone was very polite but I noticed his father was absent.

Cross was engaged in an intense conversation with one of his uncles when I felt someone sneak up on me while I was at the bar ordering an orange juice and ginger ale mix.

"Mmmm looking good Charly Brinx."

I rolled my eyes before turning around. Shit! I knew that voice. I turned slowly to see

Luca standing there.

"I'm surprised to see you here." Luca said, burning a hole into my breasts.

"Why? I'm right where I'm supposed to be, here with my husband. This party is for us."

"Your husband? Curtis Jr. told me this was his going away party. He didn't mention you and Croccifixio had gotten married." Luca's entire face seemed to have twisted up. "The two of you are really married?"

"Yes, we are." Cross confirmed for the disbelievers, coming out of nowhere and draping his arm around me.

"Croccifixio." Luca greeted him halfheartedly.

"Luca."

For a few awkward seconds there was a stare down between the two men.

"What's up Luca!" Curtis Jr. stepped in. "Thanks for coming."

"Thanks for the invite." Luca said, cutting his eyes at me.

Cross clinched his jaw and I knew he was getting mad. "Let's go dance, baby." I pulled him away and led him to the dance floor.

I threw my arms around my husband and we moved our bodies in sync, to the slow beat blaring out the speakers. I wanted to get his mind off Luca because there was no need for Cross to cut a fool in here over some bullshit.

On our way off of the dance floor Cross stopped. I looked at him and followed his eyes. Cadence and Kayla stood there talking to no other than Cross's father. The girls wanting to be grown, had arrived earlier in Cadence car. Cross tightened the grip on my hand as we walked over.

"Cross, Charly." Curtis Sr. welcomed us.

"Pop." I could hear a cautiousness in Cross's voice.

"Hello, Curtis." I hadn't talked to this man in years and here I was standing face to face with my Godfather and my dad's arch enemy.

"The two of you have a beautiful daughter. Cross she looks a lot like you. You did good, son." Curtis Sr. smiled as if he was proud.

"Charly, you did an excellent job raising her." Curtis Sr. nodded his head agreeing with his own statement.

"Thank you." I faked a smile, not believing any form of a compliment from this man was sincere.

"Is she as feisty as you were?" Curtis Sr.

watched Cadence intently.

"No!!!!!!" Cross and I said at the same time. We all started to laugh.

"Well, I can't wait for your mother to meet her. Seeing those two girls, just might be what she needs."

"I agree." Cross said to him.

"We're having a Sunday dinner at the house. I hope you and the family can make it." Curtis Sr. looked at me while he spoke.

"We'll be there." I smiled, not yet trusting him but appreciating the effort Curtis Sr. was making.

"I never realized how much you look like your mother. She was a good woman."

"Thanks for saying that."

The rest of the night was uneventful until my own father showed up. I thought my heart stopped for a second. I didn't believe he was going to show up. "Baby, can you excuse me for a second. My dad just got here."

"If it ain't Charlie Brinx in the flesh," Crossed grinned as if he was happy to see my father. I know I was. "Yeah, you go speak to your dad. I need to go find Santi. Stay strong, my love. You know I got you." Cross gently kissed me, before I went on my way.

"Daddy, you came!" We held each other tightly.

"What you said to me really hit home. I can't remember the last time I've seen you cry. I always told you, tears were a sign of weakness but you never looked more strong than when you asked me to accept Cross as your husband. I'm proud to call you my daughter."

"Daddy, I love you so much."

"I know you do but guess what?"

"What?"

"I love you even more."

"I hate to break up this father/daughter moment but I wanted to take this opportunity to see if I can make this night, even more magical than it already is," Francesco stated, standing next to me and daddy with Curtis Sr. right beside him.

Daddy and Curtis Sr. stood facing each other. I was praying they didn't start exchanging blows in the midst of the party.

"I'm the head of this organization but more importantly, I'm the heart of this family," Francesco stated as if it was fact, although I felt his statement was up for debate. But if he could bring peace between my dad and Curtis Sr., I was willing to go along with whatever he said.

"Is that right." Daddy seemed unimpressed by what Francesco said but I was hoping he would continue to listen instead of shutting down.

"I made one promise to myself before I came here tonight."

"What promise was that?" daddy wanted to know.

"I said if you and Curtis Sr. both showed up, I would do everything in my power to reunite the two men who were once the best of friends. Charile," Francesco nodded then turned his attention to Curtis Sr. "None of us are getting any younger. Charly and Cross who both run your operations are now husband and wife. It's time for both of you to leave your animosity in the past so we can build our future. Will the both of you do that for me?"

Daddy and Curtis Sr. both remained silent. Neither one was willing to make the first step towards healing. It was breaking my heart. But then Curtis Sr. glanced over at Cadence and Kay-la her dancing with each other. Laughing and having a wonderful time. Their hearts were still pure and not jaded by the bad blood between the families. I believe seeing that, softened Curtis Sr.

"I'm willing to try if Charlie is." They say it only takes one to heal a nation. I'm not sure how true that is but I do know, with Curtis Sr.'s gesture, he healed my daddy's cold heart.

"I'm willing to try too. Can we talk...man to man?" Charlie asked.

"I would love to but not in this loud ass place!" Curtis Sr. cracked. "I can barely hear myself think," he joked and we all laughed.

"My limo is parked right outside. My driver will let you in and the two of you can have all the privacy you need," Francesco offered. "I know you both have a lot to sort out, so take all the time you need."

"Sounds good!" I watched something I never thought I'd live to see in my life. Daddy and Curtis Sr., walking out together, having a meaningful conversation and I even noticed daddy cracking a smile.

"Francesco, I will forever be grateful for what you did here tonight. This feud between our fathers is finally coming to an end and it's all thanks to you."

"Charly, it's because of you and Cross too. Those two men are as stubborn as they come but what they mutually share is their undying love for family. This is a beautiful thing, my dear."

"Francesco, what you still doing here?" Curtis Jr. came out of nowhere and asked.

"I was about to leave but when I saw Charlie Brinx arrive, I decided to stay and see if I could get him and your father to mend their broken friendship."

"And did you?"

"Yes!" Francesco was clearly pleased with himself. "At this point, I'm sure they're knee deep in their conversation."

"Hmm, I guess yo' sneaky ass is good for something," I heard Curtis Jr. mumble under his breath. Thank goodness I was standing the closest to Jr. and it was so loud in the venue, Francesco didn't peep what the oldest Payne brother said. I shook my head, stunned at how bold Jr. was being.

"I better go find Cross and tell him the good news. It was good seeing you Francesco and thanks again," I said giving him a hug.

"You welcome my beautiful, Charly. This is an exciting new chapter for the entire organization. Now excuse me. I'm going to have a seat and wait for Charlie and Curtis to rejoin us," Francesco said, walking away.

"Rejoin us...where the fuck they go?" Jr. questioned.

"Oh, it was so loud in here, Francesco let daddy and Curtis Sr. talk things out in his limo."

In a blink of an eye, all the color drained from Curtis Jr. face. He brushed past me with such a swiftness, the air damn near knocked me over.

"Where the fuck is Curtis running off to?!" Cross walked up to me looking disheveled. "Don't even tell me. I just wanna get the fuck up outta here."

"Baby, what's going on? You look like you ready to kill somebody." Before Cross could respond, Santi came flying past us, yelling at the top of his lungs for Jr. to stop.

"No need to chase Jr. down. That nigga can't save you," Cross remarked as we headed towards the exit.

"Yo, Cross!" I stopped him in his tracks. "Tell me what the fuck is going on! All three of you Payne brothers are acting bat shit crazy. Even more so than usual."

"I'll tell you when we get in the car!" he barked, picking up his speed in a hurry to get to the exit. I was trailing close behind, trying to figure out how less than thirty minutes ago, shit was lovely. Now Cross, Santi and Curtis Jr. all had the dreaded look of death plastered across their faces.

"Cross, slow down!" I shouted, wanting him to wait up for me. "Damn, I'm your wife! We came together, we leaving together too," I snapped.

"Baby, I apologize." He reached out his hand and grabbed mine. "Forgive me." Cross kissed my cheek as he opened the door. Right as we stepped through the double doors, what sounded like a bomb exploding filled the air. The next thing I remember, was everything fading to black.

The Funeral...

Cross and I held hands as the caskets were lowered into the ground. Both of our fathers died in the car explosion and we decided it was only right they were buried next to each other.

Especially given their long history as friends, then becoming mortal enemies to finally, after all these years putting the past behind them and embracing on the night they were killed. Cross placed a shovel of dirt on the top of his father's casket and I threw a white rose on daddy's casket.

Curtis Jr. also died in the explosion but since he was the one responsible, we decided to let the mother of his children handle the funeral arrangements and not attend. His intended target was Francesco but of course that shiesty old man had nine lives and escaped harm. That's the reason Curtis Jr. was rushing to get to Francesco's limo when I told him his father and my dad were in his car. He tried to save their lives but it was too late. Santi also became a casualty in Curtis Jr.'s ill-conceived plan to take out Francesco before going away to prison.

"First Tia, now my daddy. I still can't believe he's gone," I said, staring out the window of the limo as it drove away from the cemetery. I took off my sunglasses and placed them on my lap, so I could wipe away the endless tears that had streamed down my face.

"We'll get through this, Charly," Cross

promised squeezing my hand.

"I appreciate you being strong for me but I know you're in just as much pain. You lost your father and both your brothers on the same night. We agreed not to attend Curtis Jr. funeral but what about Santi? You all were so close. We should be there, Cross."

Cross shifted his body and let go of my hand. "Charly, I wanted to wait and tell you this because you're still grieving for your father but you need to know."

"Need to know what? I turned in my seat to face Cross. He was wearing his sunglasses but I took them off. His eyes were red but they weren't filled with sadness, it seemed more like anger and pain. "Cross, talk to me. What do you have to tell me?"

'Tia's car crash wasn't an accident," Cross stated.

I gave him a baffled stare. "I don't understand. The police said she had been drinking. There was an open bottle of wine in her car. She was drunk. Lost control of the wheel and her car went over the bridge. The police wouldn't make that up!"

"They were led to believe that's what happened."

"Led to believe...by who and why?"

"By Santi. Santi murdered Tia and set it up to look like an accident."

"No! Why would Santi do that?! He loved Tia and she loved him!" I yelled.

"Baby, keep your voice down." Cross then eyed the limo driver. "Roll up the partition please. You don't need to be getting so upset. You have to think about the baby."

"You're not making any sense!" My voice was shaky. This all seemed like too much. "The baby is fine. Now answer me! Why would Santi kill Tia?" I demanded to know.

"Because she overheard him talking to the men he hired to kill you. When you and Tia got shot at that day, it was all Santi."

My eyes widened in disbelief. "Why?" was all I managed to get out. I was too stunned to say anything else. My mind instantly went back to the missed calls and text message I got from Tia on the night she died. Santi played it off that he had asked for Tia's hand in marriage but she was on her way to tell me the truth about what he had done.

"Santi figured if he could get you out my life permanently, he would gain favor with our father. I always thought Curtis Jr. was the only one who wanted to take over the family business. Come to find out, Santi had his eye on the prize the entire time. He betrayed all of us." Cross let out a deep sigh as if he'd unloaded a heavy burden.

"When did you find out?"

"The night of the party. I walked up on him and Curtis Jr. having a heated argument. I wanted to know what the fuck was going on. Curtis Jr. spilled it all before storming off. I guess he had other things on his mind, like blowing up Francesco's limo with him in it," Cross shook his head.

"Unfuckin' believable." My sadness completely shifted to fury. Now I wished Santi hadn't died in the explosion so I could kill him myself.

"You think you know someone and then you realize they're a complete stranger. All these years I was wary of the wrong brother."

"You and me both. I thought Santi was a good guy but that nigga wanted me dead. Then he killed my best friend...my sister. I can only imagine how devastated Tia must've been, when she realized the man she was in love with, was the devil in disguise. Talk about lovin' the enemy." I leaned back in my seat and closed my eyes.

"Luckily we're gettin' out the game and putting all this bullshit behind us," Cross said, sounding relieved.

"Fuck that! We ain't going nowhere. Tia and my daddy didn't die in vain." I held on tightly to Cross's hand. "We will run this organization together as husband and wife. You my ride or die now. You're all I need." I held up Cross's hand and kissed his wedding band, as we drove off to begin a new chapter in our life together.

Coming Soon

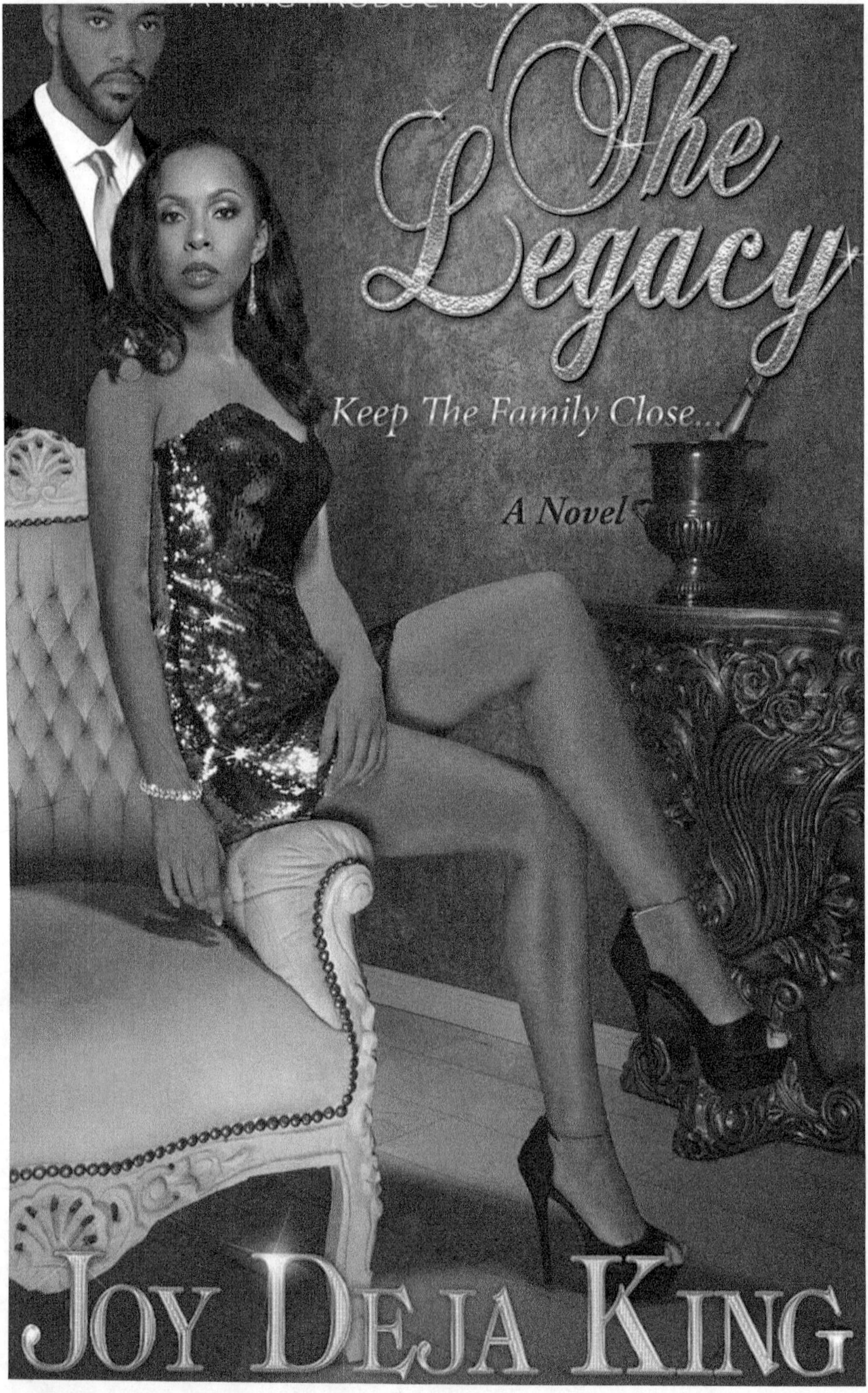
The Legacy
Keep The Family Close...
A Novel
JOY DEJA KING

Chapter One

Raised By Wolves

"Alejo, we've been doing business for many years and my intention is for there to be many more. But I do have some concerns..."

"That's why we're meeting today," Alejo interjected, cutting Allen off. I've made you a very wealthy man. You've made millions and millions of dollars from my family..."

"And you've made that and much more from our family," Clayton snapped, this time being the one to cut Alejo off. "So let's acknowledge this being a mutual beneficial relationship between both of our families."

Alejo slit his eyes at Clayton, feeling disrespected, his anger rested upon him. Clayton was the youngest son of Allen Collins but also the most vocal. Alejo then turned towards his son Damacio who sat calmly not saying a word in his father's defense, which further enraged the dictator of the Hernandez family.

An ominous quietness engulfed the room as the Collins family remained seated on one side of the table and the Hernandez family occupied the other.

"I think we can agree that over the years we've created a successful business relationship that works for all parties involved," Kasir said, speaking up and trying to be the voice of reason and peacemaker for what was quickly turning into enemy territory. "No one wants to create new problems. We only want to fix the one we currently have so we can all move forward."

"Kasir, I've always liked you," Alejo said with a half smile. "You've continuously conducted yourself with class and respect. Others can learn a lot from you."

"Others, meaning your crooked ass nephews," Clayton barked not ignoring the jab Alejo was taking at him. He then pointed his finger at Felipe and Hector, making sure that everyone at the table knew exactly who he was speaking of since there were a dozen family members on the Hernandez side of the table.

Chaos quickly erupted within the Hernandez family as the members began having a heated exchange amongst each other. They were speaking Spanish and although neither Allen nor Clayton understood what was being said, Kasir spoke the language fluently.

"Dad, I think we need to fall back and not let this

meeting get any further out of control. Let's table this discussion for a later date," Kasir told his father in a very low tone.

"Fuck that! We ain't tabling shit. As much money as we bring to this fuckin' table and these snakes want to short us. Nah, I ain't having it. That shit ends today," Clayton stated, not backing down.

"You come here and insult me and my family with your outrageous accusations," Alejo stood up and yelled, pushing back the single silver curl that kept falling over his forehead. "I will not tolerate such insults from the likes of you. My family does good business. You clearly cannot say the same."

"This is what you call good business," Clayton shot back, placing his iPhone on the center of the table. Then pressing play on the video that was sent to him.

Alejo grabbed the phone from off the table and watched the video intently, scrutinizing every detail. After he was satisfied he then handed it to his son Damacio, who after viewing, passed it around to the other family members at the table.

"What's on that video?" Kasir questioned his brother.

"I want to know the same thing," his father stated.

"Let's just say that not only are those two motherfuckers stealing from us, they're stealing from they own fuckin' family too," Clayton huffed, leaning back in his chair, pleased that he had the proof to back up his claims.

"We owe your family an apology," Damacio said, as his father sat back down in his chair with a glaze of defeat in his eyes. It was obvious the old man hated to be wrong and had no intentions of admitting it, so his son had to do it for him.

"Does that mean my concerns will be addressed and handled properly?" Allen Collins questioned.

"Of course. You have my word that this matter will be corrected in the very near future and there is no need for you to worry, as it won't happen again. Please accept my apology on behalf of my entire family," Damacio said, reaching over to shake each of their hands.

"Thank you, Damacio," Allen said giving a firm handshake. "I'll be in touch soon."

"Of course. Business will resume as usual and we look forward to it," Damacio made clear before the men gathered their belongings and began to make their exit.

"Wait!" shouted Alejo. The Collins men stopped in their tracks and turned towards him.

"Father, what are you doing?" Damacio asked, confused by his sudden outburst.

"There is something that needs to be addressed and no one is leaving this room until it's done," Alejo demanded.

With smooth ease, Clayton rested his arm towards the back of his pants, placing his hand on the Glock 20–10mm auto. Before the meeting, the Collins' men had agreed to have their security team wait outside in the parking lot instead of coming in the building, so it wouldn't be a hostile environment. But that didn't stop Clayton from taking his own precautions. He eyed his brother Kasir who maintained his typical calm demeanor that annoyed the fuck out of Clayton.

"Alejo, what else needs to be said that wasn't already discussed?" Allen asked, showing no signs of distress.

"Please, come take a seat," Alejo said politely. Allen stared at Alejo then turned to his two sons and nodded his head as the three men walked back towards their chairs.

Alejo wasted no time and immediately began his over the top speech. "I was born in Mexico and raised by wolves. I was taught that you kill or be killed. When I rose to power by slaughtering my enemies and my friends, I felt no shame," Alejo stated, looking around at everyone sitting at the table. His son Damacio swallowed hard as his Adam's apple seemed to be throbbing out of his neck.

"As I got older and had my own family, I decided I didn't want that for my children. I wanted them to understand the importance of loyalty, honor, and respect," Alejo said proudly, speaking with his thick Spanish accent, which was heavier than usual. He moved away from his chair and began to pace the floor as he spoke. "Without understanding the meaning of being loyal, honoring, and respecting your family, you're worthless. Family forgives but some things are unforgivable so you have no place on this earth or in my family."

Then, without warning and before anyone had even noticed, blood was squirting from Felipe's slit throat. With the same precision and quickness, Alejo took his sharp pocketknife and slit Hector's throat too. Everyone was too stunned and taken aback to stutter a word.

Alejo wiped the blood off his pocketknife on the white shirt that a now dead Felipe was wearing. He kept wiping until the knife was clean. "That is what happens when you are disloyal. It will not be tolerated... ever." Alejo made direct contact with each of his family members at the round table before focusing on Allen. "I want to personally apologize to you and your sons. I do not condone what Felipe and Hector did and they have now paid the price with their lives."

"Apology accepted," Allen said.

"Yeah, now let's get the fuck outta here," Clayton whispered to his father as the three men stood in unison, not speaking another word until they were out the building.

"What type of shit was that?" Kasir mumbled.

"I told you that old man was fuckin' crazy," Clayton said shaking his head as they got into their waiting SUV.

"I think we all knew he was crazy just not that crazy. Alejo know he could've slit them boys' throats after we left," Allen huffed. "He just wanted us to see the fuckin' blood too and ruin our afternoon," he added before chuckling.

"I think it was more than just that," Clayton replied, looking out the tinted window as the driver pulled out the parking lot.

"Then what?" Kasir questioned.

"I think old man Alejo was trying to make a point, not only to his family members but to us too."

"You might be right, Clayton."

"I know I'm right. We need to keep all eyes on Alejo 'cause I don't trust him. He might've killed his crooked ass nephews to show good faith but trust me that man hates to ever be wrong about anything. What he did to his nephews is probably what he really wanted to do to us but he knew nobody would've left that building alive. The only truth Alejo spoke in there was he was raised by wolves," Clayton scoffed leaning back in the car seat.

All three men remained silent for the duration of the drive. Each pondering what had transpired in what was supposed to be a simple business meeting that turned into a double homicide. They also thought about the point Clayton said Alejo was trying to make. No one wanted that to be true as their business with the Hernandez family was a lucrative one for everyone involved. But for men like Alejo, sometimes pride held more value than the almighty dollar, which made him extremely dangerous.

P.O. Box 912
Collierville, TN 38027

www.joydejaking.com
www.twitter.com/joydejaking

A King Production

ORDER FORM

Name:

Address:

City/State:

Zip:

QUANTITY	TITLES	PRICE	TOTAL
	Bitch	$15.00	
	Bitch Reloaded	$15.00	
	The Bitch Is Back	$15.00	
	Queen Bitch	$15.00	
	Last Bitch Standing	$15.00	
	Superstar	$15.00	
	Ride Wit' Me	$12.00	
	Ride Wit' Me Part 2	$15.00	
	Stackin' Paper	$15.00	
	Trife Life To Lavish	$15.00	
	Trife Life To Lavish II	$15.00	
	Stackin' Paper II	$15.00	
	Rich or Famous	$15.00	
	Rich or Famous Part 2	$15.00	
	Rich or Famous Part 3	$15.00	
	Bitch A New Beginning	$15.00	
	Mafia Princess Part 1	$15.00	
	Mafia Princess Part 2	$15.00	
	Mafia Princess Part 3	$15.00	
	Mafia Princess Part 4	$15.00	
	Mafia Princess Part 5	$15.00	
	Boss Bitch	$15.00	
	Baller Bitches Vol. 1	$15.00	
	Baller Bitches Vol. 2	$15.00	
	Baller Bitches Vol. 3	$15.00	
	Bad Bitch	$15.00	
	Still The Baddest Bitch	$15.00	
	Power	$15.00	
	Power Part 2	$15.00	
	Drake	$15.00	
	Drake Part 2	$15.00	
	Female Hustler	$15.00	
	Female Hustler Part 2	$15.00	
	Female Hustler Part 3	$15.00	
	Female Hustler Part 4	$15.00	
	Female Hustler Part 5	$15.00	
	Princess Fever "Birthday Bash"	$9.99	
	Nico Carter The Men Of The Bitch Series	$15.00	
	Bitch The Beginning Of The End	$15.00	
	Supreme...Men Of The Bitch Series	$15.00	
	Bitch The Final Chapter	$15.00	
	Stackin' Paper III	$15.00	
	Men Of The Bitch Series And The Women Who Love Them	$15.00	
	Coke Like The 80s	$15.00	
	Baller Bitches The Reunion Vol. 4	$15.00	
	Stackin' Paper IV	$15.00	
	The Legacy	$15.00	
	Lovin' Thy Enemy	$15.00	

Shipping/Handling (Via Priority Mail) $6.75 1-2 Books, $8.95 3-4 Books add $1.95 for ea. Additional book.

Total: $_____FORMS OF ACCEPTED PAYMENTS: Certified or government issued checks and money Orders, all mail in orders take 5-7 Business days to be delivered